ESTHER STORIES

Peter Orner

ESTHER STORIES

A Mariner Original

HOUGHTON MIFFLIN COMPANY

BOSTON / NEW YORK / 2001

Copyright © 2001 by Peter Orner

For information about permission to reproduce selections from this book,
write to Permissions, Houghton Mifflin Company, 215 Park Avenue South,
New York, New York 10003.

Visit our Web site: www.houghtonmifflinbooks.com.

Library of Congress Cataloging-in-Publication Data
Orner, Peter.
  Esther stories / Peter Orner.
    p. cm.
  "A Mariner original."
  ISBN 0-618-12873-5
    1. United States—Social life and customs—20th century—Fiction.
2. Jewish families—Fiction. 3. Domestic fiction, American. I. Title.
PS3615.R58 E88 2001
816'.6—dc21   2001024991

The author gratefully acknowledges the editors of the following publications, where
some of these stories first appeared in slightly different form: *Atlantic Monthly* ("The
Raft"); *Atlantic Unbound* ("The House on Lunt Avenue"); *Cream City Review*
("County Road G" and "At the Motel Rainbow"); *Denver Quarterly* ("In the Walls");
Epoch ("Shoe Story" and "Providence"); *North American Review* ("Cousin Tuck's,"
"Sitting Theodore," and "Two Poes"); *Passages North* ("Papa Gino's"); *Michigan
Quarterly Review* ("Walt Kaplan Reads *Hiroshima*, March 1947"); *Oxford Review*
("Thumbs"); *Southern Review* ("Melba Kuperschmid Returns" and "Initials Etched
on a Dining-Room Table, Lockeport, Nova Scotia"); *Yankee* ("Awnings, Bedspreads,
Combed Yarns"). "In the Walls" also appeared in a limited-edition collection called
Seep (Sierras Press, 1998). "The Raft" was reprinted in *The Best American Short Stories
2001* and "Melba Kuperschmid Returns" in *The Pushcart Prize XXVI*.

The excerpt from *Hiroshima* by John Hersey, copyright © 1947 by John Hersey,
is reprinted by permission of Random House, Inc.

Book design by Melissa Lotfy
Typefaces: Adobe Garamond, Perpetua

Printed in the United States of America
QUM 10 9 8 7 6 5 4 3 2 1

To my brother, Eric,

AND

In memory of Andre Dubus

Contents

I have spoken of the origin, progress, and present condition of this new and thriving place. But notwithstanding these ever falling waters, and these granite buildings, and all this iron machinery, and everything that looks so strong and permanent around us, the time may come when this village shall be raised from its deepest foundations. Where are the people of former ages?

—Reverend Orin Fowler, *History of Fall River, Massachusetts,* 1841

I.

WHAT REMAINS

Initials Etched on a Dining-Room Table, Lockeport, Nova Scotia

T HE GIRL was young when she did it, and she didn't live there. This was in 1962. She was eighteen. She'd been hired to tidy the place. It was three, maybe four years before anybody noticed. The letters were so small, and they always ate in the kitchen. And when they did discover them, she was already gone to Halifax. By that time the girl had a reputation to escape from. So when they put two and two together and figured out it was she that did it, they weren't surprised. Of course she'd be the one to do something like this, they said—shameless girl, not shocking at all.

A cod fisherman, a captain, lived in the house with his wife, one of the original Locke mansions on Gurden Street overlooking the harbor. They never had children, but dust collects nonetheless in a house so huge. The girl had never been in a place that grand. At least that's what they told each other when they found her letters. *RGL.* That she'd wanted to leave her mark in the world, something that would last, something that would stay. The family still lived in town, her father and brothers sold hardware, so they could have held somebody accountable for the damage if they'd wanted to. But the captain and his wife talked it over and decided not to mention it to anyone. Not that they approved—Lord no. It was defacement of property. Vandalism. Of course it was an heirloom; it had belonged to her mother's mother, a burnished mahogany drop-leaf built in York in 1844. They could never approve. But they were quiet people; they kept to themselves in the hard times, and even in the good times they held their distance. Besides, what could anybody do about it now? What was done was done. Still, that didn't mean the captain's wife didn't watch more carefully over the other girls who came to clean, and it didn't mean the captain didn't sometimes think of her sugar breath, that morning, the one out of a thousand when he was home and slept late—he'd startled her in the kitchen. *Captain Adelbert! I didn't have any idea you were home, me banging the pots down here to wake the dead.* His only intention was to touch her sweater (Lucy was out, still teaching school then), but he couldn't stop and kissed her, her hands at her sides. She didn't resist or desire, and that had made him a fool for years.

Yet over the longer years—when the fish became scarcer, when they'd long since failed their vow to fill that house with children, when the silences between them sometimes lasted hours, when the captain's wife no longer paced the house, waiting for him, or word of him—an odd thing. They still talked about the letters. *RGL* became a part of the table that had always been too good to eat on, as important as the deep swirls carved at the top of the legs. She. The simple fact of her once among them, among their things, dusting, opening closet doors, tracing her finger along the frames of the paintings in the front room. Taking a needle—she must have used a needle—and climbing up on the table, walking on her knees to a spot just off the center.

In the dark, now older, now retired, still in the house, they murmur: "She was a pretty girl, wasn't she?"

"Curls. Yes, yes. Got in trouble with the boys early on, didn't she?"

"What do you think the G stands for?"

"Gina? Gertrude?"

"Georgette?"

"Never came back here ever."

"No, never heard of it. Family acts like she never existed."

"Well. She was a disgrace, I suppose."

"Yes, well."

They both think of her. Sleep comes slowly. Now the captain coughs and twists. Age and too much time on land have made him restless, a man who was never restless, a man who had always slept the unmovable sleep of beached whales, now tossing and muttering, waking with sweat-wet hands, afraid. Now he dreams of drowning. And the captain's wife stares at the ceiling in the dark and thinks of leading a child, Rachel Larsh's child, an angry boy in new leather shoes, through the house, pointing out the captain's trophies, the swordfish he caught during that trip to the Pacific (on the wall in the library), the hidden staircase behind the summer kitchen, and here, see, look, beneath the vase he brought back from St. John, your mother's initials. And the boy not curious, shaking free his hand.

Thumbs

T HEY FOUND HIM the same afternoon they found her (two days after her husband discovered her car in the parking lot of a supermarket in Galesburg). He was leaning against the ruins of an old corncrib, still weeping, his head between his knees. He'd broken both his thumbs in a rusty hinge. When they bandaged them up at the jail in Aledo, his thumbs were black.

Out near New Boston, Illinois, floods are so common that the land is soggy no matter what the season. Even so, people say the Mississippi moves slower in their part of the western edge of the state. To honor their dead towns, they say. Industry, except of course John Deere (you can't kill John Deere, people say), has long since moved south, and even north, anywhere but here. In 1958, the National Park Service described New Boston as "a charming old town originally laid out by Abraham Lincoln when he was junior surveyor at New Salem." Now a single store remains open on Center Street, a Casey's Minimart, and if you want a tour of the museum (on the first floor of what used to be the Lincoln House Hotel) you can call one of two numbers written on a cardboard sign tacked to the front door and ask for either Debbie

Shambrock or Eleanor Lloyd. On the river, at the end of the town pier, there's a floating gas station for fishermen where you can buy Pepsi, ice, and lures. In the other direction, along route A-27 where it intersects the Great River Road, are the remains of an old Greek-revival mansion, grass growing up between the steps, the pillars gnawed like tossed-away corncobs.

Lock Dam Road is a gravel road that looks like many others northwest of town. It is not marked and the name appears only on the most detailed regional map, a map the sheriff had to consult before he informed the press where the body was found. He couldn't have just said they found her in a hollowed-out tree in a field on the land Steve Matovic used to rent before he split up with his wife and stopped farming altogether. That wouldn't have meant much to the out-of-town press. Unlike the other roads, which all fork, Lock Dam Road holds and eventually hits the river. At the end of it is Lock Dam #3, which the state stopped operating in 1975. The tree, which is about a mile from the river, stands alone and must for years have been a favorite target of the lightning that did finally get it. One jagged portion remains, blackened, a charred finger pointing up. People say it looked like a grave even before it happened. High school kids for years used it as a dump for empties.

Mostly it was the old naggy curiosity that made her drive out there. When she was a kid she would leap on her bike at the sound of a siren anywhere near her house and investigate until she found the fire trucks or ambulance or cops. And then sometimes she'd wait an hour or so for something to happen, even though usually it didn't amount to much more excitement than the paramedics wheeling out an already stiff old cooter or, at other, rarer times, someone younger. The only noise the rattle of the gurney's crazy wheels across the asphalt and the jounce of the fluid bottles above the head of the silent main event. She drove south to New Boston from a suburb of Davenport, Iowa. She crossed the river at Muscatine. Her name was Janet, and she was a senior in high school, already accepted into college at Ames. She had her own car, so she didn't have to tell anybody where she was going. And if anybody asked, she would have lied, because what would people have thought if she told them she wanted to see the tree where they found the teacher that got hacked, the mother with the three kids. Her friends would call her completely morbid; her mother would call her lazy. She'd read about it in the Quad Cities paper. EX-STUDENT HELD IN TEACHER MURDER. Travis Oarly. No criminal record. Eight years ago he'd been a student in her class. He was known as being maybe a little slow, but never violent. The paper quoted a neighbor, who said he'd never so much as spat on a plant all the eighteen years she'd known him. "Travis was always gentle. He never said much after his mother died, but even so he smiled at you. I'm floored by this. A thing like this you can't get yourself to believe." The corncrib where they found him was three hundred yards away from the tree. They found his truck in a creek a mile southwest. And then there was that stuff about the thumbs, which the paper said the police were still investigating. The article quoted the county public defender, who hinted, though he insisted it was far too early to speculate, that the condition of his client's thumbs "indicates the strong possibility of third-party involvement."

It was after 8:30 on a Wednesday night when she stopped

at the Casey's for directions. The woman behind the counter had a kind, supple face and wiggly arms. When Janet pushed the door open, the chimes thwacked the glass and the woman appeared to wake from a nap she was taking while standing. Janet could tell from the way her jaw drooped a bit and then tightened that she was curious why a girl not from around here would want to go poking around Lock Dam Road at night, especially after what had happened out there not even ten days ago. But she kept it to herself, only gave directions as best she could. Janet nodded vigorously and pretended to understand. Then she bought a Coke and a chocolate doughnut and thanked her a lot. It was still light, the second week of May, but as she walked back to the car Janet could feel the heat of the day leaving quickly, as though draining into the river she could feel lurking down there at the end of the street.

She kept getting lost, driving to the last houses of dead ends. Kept backing up into driveways and turning around and trying other roads. It took another half hour before she found it, and even then she wasn't sure until it kept going— twisting, then sharp-angling—four miles or so. The tree was easy to spot, all alone out there. By this time it was less dark than simply ash-colored, with streaks of white-gray light low in the trees that hid the river. She parked on the edge of the road and walked across the boggy ground. There was a strand of yellow POLICE LINE DO NOT CROSS tape bunched up on the ground. It looked like a leftover streamer. Other than that, no sign of what had happened there, only bootprints turned puddles in the mud. Standing before the tree, she thought about how perfectly innocent places take on meanings they don't deserve: the empty lot where her grandfather's store burned down (the rumors that he set the fire himself made the black cement remains of the basement even worse to look at); the spot near the Dumpster behind the granary where her sister did a bump of crystal meth and then almost got raped by Derrick Fanton's brother Ty; the intersection of Gurlick and Seventh, where Maury Ravel got squashed. She figured the tree used to be an elm, but she really didn't know. Maybe it was a sycamore. She'd always meant to get a tree book, but whenever she went to the library for things like that, she always ended up getting distracted by the towers of newspapers in the periodical room. She knocked on the bark and it felt wet against her knuckles. Inside, there was soil mixed with clean white gravel. With the bark pointing to the sky like that, the tree looked like a huge high-back dining-room chair. The opening wasn't facing the road, so whoever found the teacher's body must have walked around from the back and looked in. She laughed at herself for being Nancy Drew and for not being afraid even though it was getting darker now. God knows, everybody would think she was nuts, but all this is is a tree. And this is only darkness. Her father, who had been afraid of everything, once told her there was so much more to be scared of than darkness, namely people. People at night, people in the early afternoon, people who laugh too much. People who don't tuck in their shirts. Her father terrified of everybody else, but when it came down to it, what had killed him started with him, spreading up from his pancreas.

They ran a picture of Travis Oarly in the paper. It was from the year he'd been a student in her class. One of those school photographers must have had a hell of a time coaxing him to smile. Him sitting before one of those godawful cloud-blue backgrounds. His cropped hair looking like some-body had cut it with a thresher. They must have made a com-promise: if Travis smiled, he got to close his eyes. His smile was more a twitch. His eyes pencil points staring out between nearly closed lids. So much retreat in those eyes it was impos-sible not to cry out for him in spite of the article that went with the picture. Well, maybe it was impossible for her not to. If her mother could hear what she was thinking, she'd say, Janet's heart bleeds for every stranger, but her hands are aller-gic to work. Feeling sorry for a killer, what about those moth-erless children? Huh, Janet? A murder in some town in Illi-nois, people you don't even know. Now let's talk about how many jobs you've quit in the past year and how many cards you never sent to Grandma Danner. You think she grows Nordstroms in the yard?

Janet sat down and leaned against the tree, felt the wet seep through her jeans. She knows he did it, that the specula-tion about other people being involved was shit, a desperate attempt by a lawyer with zero to divert attention from the obvious. The newspaper passed it on to sell more papers. Fool cops and lawyers, reporters—any answer you want's right there in the school picture. Anybody with half an ounce of humanity would have been kind to a boy who couldn't force himself to look out his own eyes, and maybe he wanted that kindness back. Or maybe he hated her for it. Janet gazed out at what she could still see of the flattened boggy fields and the cluster of abandoned farm buildings. Somewhere over there stood the corncrib where they found him. The rusting equip-ment, blacker shadows against the darkening gray. To the east, behind her, the rectangled light of a single inhabited trailer in the distance across the fields. Soon the sky and the ground will turn the same dull black, the color of the tree it-self. I won't go back to the car, she whispered. Not yet. She took off her shoes and rubbed them in the soft slick of mud.

She thought of his seeing her, after so many years, seeing her.

Everything's lonely today. Even his hands on the wheel are lonely today.

(And her mother asking quietly, but really shouting from the trees and darkness, What in God's name does any of this have to do with you?)

White tennis shoes in the parking lot. And his jarring the door open and her leaning in to say hi, to shake his hand and say, It's good to see you, Travis—and his taking that hand and yanking, the groceries falling, crushing bananas, a box of Cream of Wheat.

Please. A voice that used to say, Try it again, Travis. Take your time, Travis. Try it again, Travis. Now the voice says, I don't know what you want. Him not knowing either. On the high-way now.

And her mother watches her mourn in the dark of a town in Illinois nobody's ever heard of—for a murderer, a cold-blooded heinous raper killer, and Janet whispers, but really shouts, Mom, the coroner found no evidence of rape. It was in the paper. Something else he wanted. She looks out into the pale nothing, the dark flat churned ground. She thinks about living here, about knowing this place well enough to see one mile different from another. She thinks of how her eyes often miss things, even in her own neighborhood. A yellow fire hydrant, paint-chipped, its foundry date 1971. A light-blue house around the corner. It took fourteen years for her to notice an old man pressing his nose to a window on the second floor. Travis knew every inch of this place. She sees him wandering here, his hands in his pockets, eyes to the ground, finding things. Steel-belted radials. Dead baby mongooses. A flooded field that looks like a swimming pool made of river. What if he only wanted to show her a pool made of river? She's lying now, but what's it matter? It's all maybe now. She thinks of what he did after to his thumbs. How the peanut-headed prosecutors—dumber even than the defense —won't see it as anything other than the incriminating (and lucky for them) remorse of an idiot. Wanted to kill your own paws for what you did? Didn't you feel so bad? Isn't that the way it went with your hands, Travis? No, something else. Out here where he stood and cried and looked at her and left her, no wind on his face, as there's none now on Janet's. Only this awful peace. Maybe he needed to feel the loss of something in his own hands. His mother died and maybe he didn't feel anything. The rusty hinge squeals and he forces it harder. He has to use his face to crush the second thumb because his other hand hurts too much. And maybe as he is doing it, maybe he also knows it won't do any good, that pain's fragile, that it vanishes fast as kindness. Maybe he knows even the hell of what he's just done to her will disappear, that he won't be able to hold it, that even his hands will heal.

In the Walls

S HE SAID she had a theory about the places she'd lived: that she carried all her old rooms around with her, and that those rooms, in a sense, were her past. She'd been adopted, and for that reason had always felt a void in the back of her eyes. All that family lore she'd never know. But, she said, the fact of her adoption prevented her from having any excuses, from being able to blame her life's failures on some baggage of the past. She'd seen too many people crippled by their family histories to want to go digging around to find out who she was, who she came from. She had the luxury of nobody coming before her. She wasn't captive. She said she'd never be captive.

But she took the rooms she had lived in around with her the way some of us lug around our grandmother's battered photo albums, leather-bound, with pictures pasted on black construction paper. She used to tell me about the room with the morning rainbow. How she'd wake up to a tiny rainbow in a corner of the ceiling. It had something to do with refracted light, the way the sun hit the window, causing particles of light to collide, smash, creating color. She said she didn't want to understand it completely. She just wanted to take it. The rainbow wasn't always there. When it was raining or cloudy or snowing, the corner trapped shadows. She said she could always tell the weather by first looking there.

Another room had a ceiling like the bottom half of a sawed-off pyramid. It was like sleeping in a coal freight car. At night in bed she'd be hauled across Nebraska through weeping crickets and dead-tired towns.

Another room, up a hill, in Spokane, was all windows, and she lived among the squirrels and the phone lines, and spent entire afternoons watching the old flowered-dress woman across the street. The woman, Helen, sitting in an unsteady folding lawn chair, crossing and recrossing her legs in a garden of tiger lilies and garbage.

She had fears. One night I woke up and found her on the floor of my room, naked, wrapped in my ratty army coat. Her eyes were wide open, but she wasn't looking at anything. She said she was afraid of the fan. The incessant whir and blur of the fan. I said I'd turn it off. No, more than the noise. It's a hateful thing. I'll throw it out the window, I said. Just please don't sleep on the floor like that.

We started staying at her place only. Her apartment was on the third floor of a rambly mansard-roofed house on Pond Street. Her room was clutter and pillows. We squeezed. I dreamed of being strangled by ivy, choking on spiked leaves. She'd scissor-kick the covers off the bed and say, Now I have you where I want you, my den, my warren. I'd show up late for work, groggy, tugging on my collar, itching.

It was a small white room with heavy drapes. I looked around for rainbows and freight cars and asked her what of this room she would carry when she left. She said she'd think of the parts of the walls that smelled like smoke and the dried blood she'd scrubbed away from a spot near the door. But also that her memory of the place was not yet formed, that it would take time, that things would come to her later.

Sometimes in the mornings she'd tell me about other rooms.

I had an efficiency in Toronto. A little girl had been raped in the closet. I used to listen to her screams in the walls. You don't believe me.

I believe you.

I'm not talking about ghosts. I'm talking about things that happened. Things that stay.

Go on. Tell me more.

At first she shrieked for only a few minutes every night. Then she started talking. That lasted longer. She kept me up at night listening to her. Sometimes she still does.

She kissed me. Then she left me in bed and went to work. I stayed there and listened and watched, waited and watched. Under the sweaty covers, I stared at the walls, tried to see laughter, moaning. Dinner-table battles, a slow caress. An old man haunted by fingers letting go of his wrist. Whose fingers? He can't remember her face. And then it was dark, and I saw a boy in nothing but a light-blue pajama top looking out between the gaps in the blinds at the retreating taillights of his mother's car. I watch him pull his hands slowly down his cheeks as he stands at the window.

Early November

S HE GOES to their tiny country house in the woods with
her young daughter, ten days after the sudden death of
her husband, and it isn't the silence but the noise, the wind in
the trees, the way the leaves whack the window. It's fall, the
height of fall, and it was a disease that took him with the
blank force of a fist pounding on a door in the dead of night.
It must have been eating away at him in secret for a long
time, maybe even last summer as he worked on screening in
this very porch, something she'd never wanted; she always
said, Who screens things in? Don't we have enough of that already? After years of this argument, she'd finally given in,
though she insisted she'd sit on the steps, that she'd never
drink her coffee in there. Now she remembers what her
mother whispered to her at the train station, and she was
only trying to be helpful. She didn't mean it the way it
sounded, but her mother had whispered, Don't lionize him,
meaning, You're young, you loved him, but don't fall so far
into grief when—eventually, her mother didn't mean tomorrow—there are men who can pull you up. Meaning: Don't
steel yourself out there. And now, standing on the porch he
destroyed, it's the noise that doesn't have the common de-
cency to wait awhile to begin.

At night she reads while her daughter sleeps. She's surprised she's able to concentrate as long as she does. It might have been a book he read, a book he may have even talked about. She can't remember things like the names of books, the names of people, the names of places. She could never remember the name of one or another town they once loved. You remember? The one with the old guy and the singing dog? Little dog not much bigger than a mouse sitting on his shoulder oooh-oooohing. Used to infuriate him, and he'd seethe, Boone, Boone, North Carolina, in the parking lot of the state park. It was in Boone and the dog's name was Rudy and the man's name was Flynn and he kept telling us that his mother had wanted to name him Errol but his father had insisted on Richard. *Richard Flynn, the guy with the dog's name was Richard Flynn.* Facts he never forgot. But he couldn't remember tilts of a head, or impressive sneezes, or the way someone once said yes by doing nothing but breathing quicker. Not for anything could he remember the droop of a chin. She puts the book down because, yes, her mind has wandered like he always said her mind wanders. The light beneath the brown shade reminds her of the dying light she saw out the train window on the way here. They always took the same train at the same time, so she knew the light, the early-November burlap light, and she might have nudged him had he been on the train, *the light,* and he would have looked at it as if he were seeing it for the first time. She leaves the lamp on, stares at it awhile before half-sleep descends.

Pile of Clothes

THE LANDLORD didn't know what to do with her clothes. The furniture he could either use or sell, but the clothes, some mothy, others pungent, mildewed, the cheap fur of one of her old coats like a cat he'd seen around a while ago. He puts on a pair of rubber gloves he found under the pipes beneath the kitchen sink, one yellow and one green, and climbs quietly, slowly, up the stairs, as if he's afraid of waking her. The her who's already been buried eight days now, at the expense of the county, in the scabbled yard out past Buffom Road, near the industrial park. He wants to run up the stairs and get this over with, but dread yanks him back, dread of opening the accordion doors of her closet. Her smell. She lived up there umpteen years; she always paid her rent on time, sliding it under the door in envelopes with scratched out return addresses. She never complained about his plumbing, about his insistence on never replacing anything with a new part when an old one would do. For years it had been easy to forget about her. Even though her feet were always peckering around up there. That and the sound of her continually moving furniture. The jolt and scrape of her tugging a bureau across the floor, an inch, then another, then another. She went out two times a day. Once for a walk in the morning and once in the afternoon, down the hill to the L'il

Peach for milk or cigarettes or an ice cream bar. The rest of her groceries were delivered. His ex-wife used to go up there and visit with her. After Ellen moved out, that was the end of that. He'd long known he had it coming to him; he never once complained about getting left to the dogs, didn't lift a finger to stop her when Ellen stood in the kitchen and wrapped exactly half the dishes and glasses in newspaper — but to abandon the old lady? When she was the only person besides the kid down at the gas station who ever talked to her? He'd meant these past two years to mount the stairs himself. He'd meant to go up there and have a chat, as Ellen used to do, maybe even apologize for driving Ellen away, out of her life as well as his, but he never got to it.

Never a louder silence than when you stand in a room where someone lived for many years alone. He looks at the clean walls; she was meticulous, but even so, her smell remains strong. A blend of trapped smoke and what? Jergen's? Burned butter left crusted on frying pans? Or simply that her body had begun to rot while she was alive up here? She never had many things. Not even a rug in the hall; only a bus schedule for the 112, long out-of-date, thumbtacked to the inside of the front door. (Where did she take the bus? Whom did she go see?) Three rooms: a kitchen, a cramped living room, mostly taken up by a couch that was once yellow but now bleached nearly white by the sun of the uncurtained window, a tiny bedroom made cave-like by the slope of the roof. He stoops and goes into the bedroom. He tries to avoid looking at the bed and fails. It is neat and hand-smoothed, except for a small furrow in the pillow. The afternoon sun has forced its way into this nook. There's a glint of a spider's thread reaching from the dresser to the window like a fishing line. Determined to stop lolling over this, he flings open the accordion doors and rams his face deep into the jackets and sweaters and coats and bear-hugs them together. Then he lifts all the clothes, as one, off the rack.

He and Ellen had been lingering forever at the kitchen table. In the bright kitchen glare of one or two in the morning (neither of them had bothered to look at a clock for hours), he stared at her warily. She'd already crumpled every bill from the basket on top of the refrigerator and flung them at him. Eastern Edison, City of Brockton (water), City of Brockton (late property tax adjustment form), Bay State Gas (urgent reply requested), New England Telephone and Telegraph, Delta Visa, another Eastern Edison, Sears Automotive, another City of Brockton. He used to call himself a restorer of houses. One year he even told people he was a "preservationist." He had loved his falling-down wrecks, his albatrosses, but he can't do the work anymore. He blames it on his knees and his lower back, but it's really this tiredness he's got. Ellen asking, always asking, "My God, what's wrong with you, man as big as you, look at the size of you." And his wanting to explain, but not knowing how, repeating, "I don't know, I don't know, I don't know." This exhaustion that no amount of sleep or coffee could defeat. And like the clutch of houses he bought so many years ago, with the money that landed in his lap from the moon—an inheritance mailed from some lawyer's office in New York City (when Ellen first said, "We can be landlords. We'll never pay rent again!")—he's letting himself go slowly to ruin. Now he sits on rents. Now he won't come to the phone when tenants call. Now he's being sued. Now he's being hailed before the Massachusetts Land Com-

mission Review Board on property-neglect charges. It's not
the bills, Ellen once said, but that you think you can live
without anybody noticing you. Even so—the notices and the
warnings were starting to kill her, and that night she was just
about to open her mouth with more bad numbers when the
old woman upstairs started pushing something across the
floor. Ellen lifted her head and listened; then suddenly she
spoke in her hushy curious voice, a voice he hadn't heard in
so long: "She's blind, you know."

"Who?"

Ellen pointed at the ceiling. "She told me the other day.
She said she'd been going that way for years, and she might as
well tell somebody it actually happened. No more sight. Just
lights and darks."

"The old bird? But she gets around fine. She's got to be
able to see something."

"Memorized. Neighborhood's all in her head. Potholes.
The aisles down at the Peach."

He looked up. "And all the redecorating?"

Ellen laughed and slid her cup toward him. Her cold coffee sloshed on the table. "I asked her finally. I figured if she
was telling me things, why not? And you know what she
said?"

"What?"

"She said if I don't make my apartment an obstacle course,
I'll forget I can't see."

"Huh?"

"I have so many pictures in my head, she said, so so many
pictures."

He took her hand and rubbed her long, thin fingers.
"How long?" he asked.

Ellen let herself look at him before she yanked her hand away.

A purple cardigan with suede elbow patches, the brown coat with the fake fur like that cat, a ragged pea coat (where the buttons used to be are now only tiny rock-hard balls of thread), a sequined dress for a much bigger woman, enclosed in plastic, a royal-blue windbreaker with yellowed lining and a union local logo on the back, skirts clipped to hangers by rusty safety pins, four moth-eaten men's suits, all charcoal gray.

Ellen had grown tomatoes and a few cucumbers in the back-yard garden. The tomatoes were the children she always in-sisted she didn't want, refused to burden the world with — she'd measure the vines as they grew up their plastic ladders and record the heights in a notebook she kept in the drawer with the car keys and matches. They'd eat them in salads, and sometimes just them, like apples. Ellen would pack up the extras in a shoe box and carry them upstairs to her.

After Ellen left, he began hearing shrieks in the night. He thought of going up there and knocking and saying, Is every-thing okay up here? I heard something. Some yelling. I was concerned. Was it you? But he never did go to her, and after a while he stopped worrying, because in the morning, as usual, he'd listen to her slow clack down the stairs right on time, be-tween 7:30 and 8:00, and she was the same as always out the window, small but not hunched, curly white hair that looped up from her shoulders like a girl's. It got to be that he'd stare at the ceiling and wait for her. The nights she didn't shriek were the worst: that old hooter sleeping peaceful, fending off whatever haunted her, and him, never more awake, listening for his own breathing.

Six-thirty on a Saturday evening in July and the St. Vincent De Paul's on Calvert Street is closed. A sign says PLEASE NO DONATIONS AFTER HOURS, but someone's already left an old computer in the seat of a baby stroller, a microwave with no door, a box of waterlogged encyclopedias, a set of Santa salt and pepper shakers, a steering wheel, a tacklebox, and a cabinet that looks like somebody shot the back out with a pellet gun. He sets the clothes in a heap on the sidewalk next to the stroller and hurries away.

Another of Ellen's ideas that they'd both believed in for a while was expanding the garden and selling their tomatoes right out of the driveway. He'd even found a good cache of lumber in the basement of one of their houses and hauled it over in the truck. He was going to build a small stand; Ellen wanted it to look like a puppet theater. The old lady upstairs was going to tend the counter on weekdays, when they were both away working. And there won't be any problems, Ellen said, because she'll figure out what to charge by the dip of the scale.

When she didn't come down in the morning and then again in the afternoon, he called the fire department and said, Something's happened to my tenant. She lives upstairs. I'm at 817 Strossen. When the two paramedics moved slowly, but absolutely, up the walk with their shoulder bags and cases and defibrillator, he handed one of them the spare key. An hour and a half later, as he stood on the lawn with the neighbors, the quiet lights of the ambulance, the two police cars, the fire truck, streaking across the windows—much more commotion that she ever made in life—they brought her down. The paramedic, the one with the sandy hair and different-color mustache, the one he'd handed the key to, stopped to talk to him. The paramedic might have asked, If you thought something wasn't right up there, why didn't you go up there and check on her? But of course he was trained not to get involved in anything personal, and God knew, he'd seen a hell of a lot stranger things on calls. For now the paramedic needed only her full name and next of kin.

"Husband deceased?"

"Yes."

"Children?"

"Not that I'm aware of."

"So no grandchildren, cousins, sisters, anything like that? Anyone else?"

"Not to my knowledge."

Sunday early morning he wakes to shrieking, and he isn't surprised that it's himself, that the hollering and carrying on is coming from his own throat. Rain pecks at the window one tap at a time, as if someone out there is trying to get his attention. He's at the bottom of the bed, in a gnarled wrestle of sheets and blanket. A place he used to find himself after long dreams when he was a kid, dreams he never remembered. But now he remembers the moment before waking, and it's a vision that sweeps his old fatigue away, even as he continues to scream at the walls of his own room: himself, kneeling on the sidewalk in the rain, weeping over those clothes.

Papa Gino's

THEY BLAME each other silently, and they've lived like this for years. Nearly a decade of silent eyeing. Here they sit at Papa Gino's on a Friday night in December, across from each other at a tiny plastic table, so close their knees touch. Neither laughs as the other wrestles drooping cheese.

Barry and Diane Swanson lost a child nine years ago. The story is simple. Barry, Diane, and Gene, who was then seven years old, were window-shopping along High Street in Dedham, Massachusetts. Gene kept bouncing a small orange rubber Superball he'd bought from a machine at Cookie's Table for a quarter. He was walking behind his parents. The ball ricocheted off a crack in the sidewalk and bounced into the street. Gene chased it. It's happened before. A blue Plymouth going too fast for High Street on a Saturday. Screech and a dull thud. Diane shrieking. Barry's already bloody hands holding Gene, and his pleading, God, please, no, no. And when eternity was over, and Barry was hovering over Gene in the back of an ambulance, Diane ran across the street and found the ball near the rim of a sewer grate. She stooped and picked it up. The slippery little ball, now worn down from years of rubbing, has remained in her purse ever since.

Barry tossed Gene the quarter to buy the ball.

Diane told him twice to stop bouncing. He was a spunky kid who'd liked to test his parents. He kept doing it. Diane did not take the ball away.

Barry was looking at a suede jacket in the window of Slaxon's, and in mid-comment about the hideousness of its color when Gene's ball sprang into the street.

The ball bounced just to the right of Diane's shoulder. Couldn't she have grabbed Gene as he bumped past her in pursuit?

Couldn't Barry have put his foot down, said enough's enough? Give me the damn ball, Gene.

Around and around and around. Four days after the funeral Barry went to work. It took Diane a full week, but then she too was back, back behind her desk at State Farm, taking calls, making referrals, seeing clients, listening to the void in her voice as she answered question after question.

Here they sit. Friday nights they eat out. They can afford better, but they feel more at ease in places like this. More anonymous. Less exposed. Silence is not wrong here. No one waits on them. Nobody chats them up. They place their orders at the counter and stand with a slip of paper that tells them their pickup number in red ink. You can see the lights of the highway from the window. I-95. The plastic tabletop has been made to look like a red-and-white-checked table-cloth. There are few sounds. The fuzzled ping-pang of a video arcade game playing itself in the corner. Muzak so low it sounds like somebody humming. Quick shout of a cook be-hind a red fake-brick wall—"Line on!" Soft yellow blankety light. Harsh if you look at the bulbs above straight on, but as a whole they combine to form a buttery glaze that drifts about the room. It is after nine and only two other tables are occupied, one by a counter girl on break. She is resting her chin on an outstretched arm and rattling her nails on the tabletop. A boy is mopping a closed section in a dark corner of the restaurant. Smell of tomato sauce and bleach. Barry and Diane eat a pepperoni with half mushrooms. Almost ten years ago, and that Saturday could just as well have been last week. Friday nights have always been tough.

They made love for a year after Gene's funeral. They made love for a year and nothing happened, nothing. They saw two doctors who told them nothing was wrong, that Diane was getting on but that all the parts were certainly in working order. "Go home and do it" is what the second doctor advised. "What else can I say?" That night they slept at the Comfort Inn, but it didn't make any difference. Then one morning, a few weeks later, Diane watched Barry come out of the shower with a towel loosely slunched around his waist, and she started to despise his body, his flubby folds, his thinning hair, his clumsy fatty hands, his sweaty naked squirming over her in the dark, like the wet glob of a seal. She could think of nothing but the man Gene would have grown into.

Barry didn't fight her. He simply watched her recoil and endured the silence. He had lost his mother when he was thirteen, and there were afternoons in the weeks following her death when he would come home from school and creep around his parents' room and steal things, a locket, an earring, even a bra once, which he kept hidden under his mattress. He was used to making do. So for years now Barry has been rubbing his big forehead, sighing, wandering the house, masturbating quietly in the bathroom, and reading.

Diane takes a sip of Diet Coke and clears her throat, but doesn't say anything. She looks at her reflection in the big window. Barry wipes his mouth with the corner of a paper napkin and slides his left hand across the table, palm up. Some nights she covers it with her own.

On a Bridge over the Homochitto

M ORE THAN HALF a lifetime away, and even now his
mind wanders back to a weekday morning on a bridge
in 1948. He was unemployed then, the only time in his
working life that he wasn't at a job on a weekday morning,
and walking along Postal Route 31 with his hands in the
pockets of his jacket, alone. Twenty-six years old and a vet-
eran, still humbled by the things he saw in Germany and
Poland at the end of the Hitler half of the war. He hadn't seen
much combat himself, but he knew then, as he knows now,
that what he saw as part of the 222nd Infantry, "The Mop-up
Crew," as he called it, could never be compared to shooting
at people or getting shot at. Human beings who didn't look
like people, shriveled hands grasping and fisting, like the tiny
fingers of dolls, and sometimes, but not always, ditches of
bodies. A place called Nordhausen, where he and another soldier found the corpse of a pregnant woman in a bloody la-
trine. An army interpreter told them that an SS had tried to
force the birth by stomping on her with his boots. He and
the other soldier, whose name he never knew, buried her. The
other soldier said a prayer, which he repeated.

A year and a half later, there he was—amazed that such a

thing as quiet could exist again in the world—rambling down Route 33 in Sibley, Mississippi, ten or so miles from his mother's place at St. Catherine Creek, in the middle of the morning. He took long walks that year, mostly to think about the things he'd seen and to get out of the house, away from his mother's hasty breathing and droning. *Someone who's done for country as you've done deserves to rest, and don't for twelve seconds believe you're lazy, or not worthy, or that you haven't done your share.* Fists jammed into pockets, surrounded by the desolation of home, the woods, the gurgle of the Homochitto River. He turns off the road and begins to cross a bridge. A simple, twin I-beam girder, wood-planked, unscuffed, about the width of a truck. Back then it was still some optimistic architect's fancy. A little bridge to nowhere really, no houses up the hill that way, just a dirt road that ended a hundred feet from the end of the bridge on the other side of the river. Beyond the end of the road, woods and a steep grade upward, what his father used to call Steve Glower's Hill. Maybe they'd planned to do some building up there, but that never came to pass.

Nothing is left now but the crumbled ruins of the two arches of a bridge that has fallen into a river.

But that morning long ago he'd stood at the railing of the little bridge, his chin resting on the backs of his hands, and looked down at the water and dreamed of a girl, not a particular girl, not one he could describe or name, but a formless one, hair and smile, quick-tongued and laughing. He saw her and didn't see her, and it was safer that way. But then, as if nudged out of the woods by the finger of God, she came out of the trees upriver, naked and white as vanilla pudding, followed closely by a man, dark-skinned, but not black, Indian maybe, naked too. For a moment the girl looked familiar, a little like his cousin Jackie, the one with all the curly sticking-up hair everybody teased her about, but this one was older than Jackie, maybe a lot older. This girl could have been thirty. It was hard to tell from up there. He watched her step fast across the rocks by the water's edge and plunge in with a wordless shout. With much more hesitation, the man followed her across the rocks and stepped off, without a peep, into the water. Neither of them looked up at the bridge. Maybe for the same reason he didn't look away. Who'd have expected the other? Who'd be standing on a bridge that didn't lead anywhere? Who'd be swimming, naked, in March? He watched her breasts float above the water; he watched the man watch her, not smiling, as though he was already counting the seconds he had left with her, with this woman who was so obviously—even from up there on the bridge—someone else's wife. (Her flailing joy in the water too free to be everyday.) Which is why both men, the man in the water and the man on bridge, stared with such useless desire. The couple didn't speak. This he remembers—cherishes, really. That neither of them succumbed to the temptation of lying about what they didn't have. Just the heavy pant and flap of swimming in the wrong season. He remembers the pressure of his erection and the awkwardness of walking away with it down the road. He remembers the man's hands as they reached out over the water and how for a single moment he wanted nothing more than to murder him so those could be his hands.

And he remembers remembering this. In 1977, driving through a snowstorm in St. Louis at 2:00 in the morning, and he's standing on the bridge. No trigger, no reason for her to come to him. Nothing in that blinding whirl to take him so far back. But there she was, amid the battering plunk of the flakes on the windshield: the way her wet hair twisted around her neck like a scarf. The sweep of her thin arms. The way she ignored men and the cold. Another time, eating with Manda and her father in some hoity-toity place in Atlanta, putting a forkful of steak in his mouth, and again, for no reason except maybe the happiness of that food, the river. Again her emergence out of the trees. His wish granted and ripped away the next moment; the dark man's head and shoulders appear. What you wish for and what you can never have— both come out of the woods at the same time. You didn't fight a war. You cleaned up after one. Still, you're your mother's hero. You don't want to work right now. You want to wander the old roads. You want to stand on the bridge and watch.

2.

THE FAMOUS

Cousin Tuck's

SHE HAD TROUBLE getting dates, so some nights she'd march into Cousin Tuck's and wait for the one-eyed man to finish playing pool. His name was Tito, and he wore a black patch over his left eye. He was a small-time hustler who could clear tables at will, using a combination of ball-smacking power and quiet, surgical, intricacy. He was also a teacher. Really more of a teacher than a hustler, because those of us who were regulars didn't dare play him for more than a few quarters a game. But lots of us would play him to learn. He'd set up your angles, a little left, a little right, pick out spots on the ball, call pockets on shots you would never have dreamed of making had he not whispered that if you hit the 13 into the right edge of the 7 with just enough oomph to bank it off the left side—*fuckdawango*—you could make that shot. Tito made you feel that you could be consistently good at the game, that you really were capable of mastering the geometry. The click of the balls as beautiful as your own heartbeat. On those nights, after four, five beers, you'd be soaring and people in the booths would start to murmur about you, point the necks of their bottles your way. You standing against the wall, chalking your cue and kissing your knuckles as if all of a sudden Cousin Tuck's was Bally's in Atlantic City and you were the guy. Everybody's guy. But on those nights Tito wasn't around, you'd be back to hitting slop, back to whacking the ball all over the table, because it was Tito who made you.

Her name was Nadine. She was very short and had a flat, almost squashed face, with a little chubbiness all over and eyes that, as Marty Patowski put it, were too big for a single head. But her heart was as wide and as long as the English High School football field across from the bar. She was our, Jamaica Plain's, locally famous community activist. This was 1987. In our humble edge of Boston, she was like a pioneer. People said that she worked as a paralegal in a legal services office, but she was known for her attendance at any and all J.P. community-based events. She'd be at the Voting Rights for Legal Aliens rally (VRLA), a featured speaker at the bi-monthly meeting of Latina Women Against AIDS Project (LWAAP), hustling money for the Youth Build summer employment program for at-risk teens in Roslindale (YBEP). You'd see her on Centre Street stapling fliers to telephone poles with that big carpenter-sized stapler she lugged around in a filthy-bottomed canvas tote bag. You'd overhear her in Woolworth's quietly grilling the cashiers—Maureen and Donna—about working conditions and insurance plans. Every time you saw her riding her bike in a wobbling rush to a meeting, you'd be reminded of all the contributions you weren't making to the betterment of society, you gluttonous hog. But Nadine never chastised. She simply tried to infect you with her enthusiasm. *Hey, I'm glad I ran into you.* Oliver or Cynthia or Fernanda or Carmen or Frankie T. *There's an interactive poetry reading tonight at St. Mary's to raise money for the Art Council's day-care center, and all you have to give is three dollars and come up with one line about what day care means to you. Oh please, nobody wants to have kids with me either. That doesn't mean Reagan's evil doesn't affect us. I'll have some ideas on notecards that I'll pass around. So just show up and you can read . . .*

Tito wouldn't make love to her. That was his rule, because he was honest about the fact that he wasn't in love with her. Admitted that even with his one eye he was a sucker for beauty and couldn't get around it, so why lie. But he'd take her home with him after the bar and hold her and kiss the scratchy backs of her arms. His bed always had clean white sheets, hotel sheets, and Nadine would feel a little guilty and decadent in that bed, the sheets slick against her bare thighs. She couldn't help thinking of all the people who would never know a bed so clean, the men and women wrapped in garbage bags sleeping in the park on Vermeer. But she usually got over it, thinking that a lot of people actually got laid once in a while, damnit, so she should be entitled to her little nibble.

On the mornings after, they'd wake up before seven, and Nadine would make a huge buttery breakfast of heaped eggs, toast, and four flavors of jam. Tito would take a run through Arnold Arb and pick up a *Globe* and a *Herald* on his way home. Then they'd sip coffee and read the news silently in Tito's immaculate kitchen. He was a printer and spent his days covered in ink, but outside of work, because of his work, Tito was fastidious, constantly scrubbing.

He taught her pool. Unlike the rest of us, no more than one-night wonders, Nadine actually had some talent. She wasn't Tito, but after a couple of weeks of lessons she was quietly clearing tables and disposing of some of the better guys

in the bar like Angel Cruz and Blake McClusky, Russell Mc-
Clusky's little nothing brother.

"She empties her eyes," Tito said. "Like Willie Mosconi
said, 'Friends, there is nothing in this world but the balls and
the pockets.' What the master meant was that you have to be
like some fool drowning. It's all blue from there. See? The
table's your ocean. Once the other stuff gets in there, once
you start noticing your opponent's fancy shoes . . . Once you
start hearing the music—even Miles's battaboop—it's over.
You're through. And Naddy's got it. Intuitively, she empties.
You don't teach that."

Nadine and Tito's story would circulate among those in
the know around the bar. How Tito taught Nadine how to
kick some ass—and that some nights he'd take her home.
Most guys gave him no grief—hell, a warm body's a warm
body. In Boston in February, there's guys who sleep with
frozen squirrel corpses. Once, when Marty Patowski said that
Tito probably put a patch over his good eye when he was de-
livering the Bob Evans home to Nadine, Sal Burkus shot him
a look so deadly that Marty coughed and took it back. "Jesus,
I joke. Can't anyone tell a joke in this friggin' place?"

Burkus pointed the rim of his beer in Marty's direction
and said, "Not you. You can't tell any jokes."

On the summer night he showed her his left eye, Tito was
standing in the doorway of the bathroom in his designer underwear. Nadine was sitting on the edge of his bed unbuttoning her blouse. He'd pulled a clean T-shirt out for her, and it
lay neatly folded on the bed beside her thigh.

"I want to see your eye," Nadine said. She'd asked before,
but she always backed off when he refused. "It's a part of you
and I want to see it."

Maybe Nadine caught Tito off guard barefoot in those silk briefs he got on sale at Filene's. It also could have been that he just figured, finally, it's only Nadine, what difference does it make if she sees? She of all people should be able to handle this. Right? Doesn't she volunteer at that nursing home on Childs Street, the place tucked back in the trees where all the inmates are old and deformed, on the edge of death, hollering into the night, a bunch of elderly lunatics clinging to their lives by yelling themselves hoarse? Doesn't she sit and read to those people and put her hand on their raving arms to calm them? So Tito shrugged and lifted the patch. He smiled. "You asked."

She couldn't conceal her revulsion. She looked down, at the clean shirt, then back at the eye. It was wreckage. A flap of skin and a gash, half an eyelid only partly covering a blurry mass of tissue, a gobble of iris and blue-white cornea.

Her reaction didn't surprise him. Tito slid the patch back down. Renee had done the same thing when he finally showed her. Had acted as if she were seeing it over and over again after he put the patch back down. Here was the same gagging look. And like Renee, Nadine was now saying something about blind people, about how much he had to be thankful for with his one good eye. It was as if someone had recorded the same bullshit Renee said and was now playing it from hidden speakers in this very room, as if Renee were under the bed. *Baby, of course you aren't any different to me now. How could I love you less?* But Renee was three years ago. She didn't leave right after. No. That would have been unseemly. But soon enough after. For a clown with two perfect shiny eyes, a greasebag assistant restaurant manager from Quincy. Tito took consolation in knowing that Renee carries the memory of his eye with her. That sometimes in bed with her tomato-sauced boyfriend, his eye floats across her night-mares like a wound.

"I'm sorry," Nadine said.

"No need."

"I bugged you." She stood up and moved closer to him, but Tito backed away. "I should have known."

"Known what?"

"That it would hurt you to show it."

"I'm not one of your causes."

"Did I say that? That you were a cause?"

"Save your bleedy heart for your social work."

Nadine stepped back to the bed, fisted the shirt, and threw it across the room. She'd promised herself when they first started leaving the bar together that this was only about being with someone, someone to help chew up the meaning-less hours when she couldn't work. That was all this was ever going to be. She turned and faced him. Stood there in her unbuttoned blouse and plum-colored bra. "And I'm some princess, Tito? You taking Princess Fergie home with you?"

"You're being stupid here now."

"You can't look at me. Easier with the light off?"

"Why don't you put the T-shirt on?"

"What if I love you?"

"Nadine. Don't—"

"For the sake of argument. Me with my big ass and this face. What if I do?"

"I told you."

"Right. That you're waiting for some ponytail to stray into the bar, a lost lamb in search of directions. Excuse me, I'm looking for the Green Street metro. Oh my!" She put her hand over her heart and swooned. "A hunky to beat all hunkies!"

"Naddy—"

"And he's Mexican! Or something like Mexican. Oh, they will be absolutely floored on Beacon Hill, floored!"

Tito retrieved the shirt from the floor and tried to hand it to her, but she refused, kept right on talking at him in that screeching voice, what the little lost girl would look like, her curls, her sneery lip, her little yellow shorts, her peek-a-boo thighs . . .

Tito watched her and listened. Her half-naked rave in the middle of his room. The rain pelted the window like a phantom tap dancer. When he tried to take her in his arms, she whapped him. "Like you're the bastard that invented loneliness."

For the first time he didn't ask her for help scratching his back, and she didn't offer. That night they slept on opposite edges of the bed. Even the bottoms of their feet didn't touch. When Tito woke up to news radio at 6:17, Nadine was long gone.

Some say they fled away together. To a cabin in backwoods Maine where they still speak French. Or maybe it was Newfoundland. San Bernardino. Others say they went separate, that she stuck to her guns and never spoke to him again, that she went to Waltham and he went to Medford. There's even one guy who swears he saw Tito doing some strange ritual dance outside her apartment, three days after she'd packed up a U-Haul and left J.P. to stew in its own juice. This guy said Tito's dance was something like half hopping and half praying, and that he kept going around and around in a circle. It all depends on how big a liar the guy who's telling it is. Because the fact is, there isn't anybody around here who knows anything more than I do. And what's it matter, really? Neither of them ever set foot back in Cousin Tuck's. What else is there?

Before they vanished, Nadine rode her bike into the bar. Pedaled right through the door. It was a hot night, and Moca Joe had propped the door open with a brick. That tote bag dangled from her handlebars. Not stopping the bike, in mid-speech about the uselessness of pool, she pedaled by our row of stools to the table, still going on about pool, how it was a disgusting waste of time and resources. Billiards! The world rides on a highway of shit while we hit glass balls into pockets like oblivious ducklings. And she called Tito all sorts of names. I won't go into all the particulars, but she let him have it as bad as she could give it, in front of all of us, in the place where he was king. She went right for his throat and said Tito's rule over Cousin Tuck's was like Reagan's, slack-jawed and drooling at the wheel while the crew cuts run the country from the basement. The pool shark racks 'em up again. Another round of opium for the masses. Then she got off the bike, let it drop, and turned to us at the bar. She said something that sounded rehearsed: "Listen up, louts. I LOVE his eye. Not his pool eye, ignorants. Do you hear me? *The eye he hides.*" She turned around and approached Tito. She placed both hands on the green felt and pulled till it ripped. Then, with one angry finger pointed at him, she said, low and vicious, as if this worst truth had only just occurred to her, "Forty-two years on earth and still dumb enough to be vain."

She got back on her bike and rode slowly toward the door. A couple of guys at the front tables moved their chairs out of the way to give her clear passage. And through the whole thing Tito just stood there holding his cue and looking at the chalk blue tip as if it were the thing exposing him, calling him out.

After Nadine coasted out of the bar (Angel stood by the door, kicked his heels together, and saluted), Tito yanked the triangle off the hook by the Bud Light girl and started to rack. He moved in the slow methodical way a shamed man does when he knows everybody's watching. His hands wandered around as though they were detached. Nobody—not even any of the newcomers, who could not have understood the significance of what had happened—stepped up to challenge. Tito broke, and the crack of the balls in the silence of the bar was enough to make even Sal Burkus wince. We listened to him knock around. He avoided the tear she'd made in the felt. Nobody made any comments. He waited a decent half hour before leaving, so we wouldn't think he was chasing her heels, her rattling back fender.

Two Poes

THEY WERE BOTH in town impersonating Edgar Poe. You'd see one or the other charge down the street in a ragged morning coat, cape, and cravat, with a similar wavy crop of unruly hair and wide forehead, but one would be silent and smiling, the other growling like something rabid. Originally, they were part of a festival honoring Poe, but the festival, after a while, became irrelevant. In time, it felt as if they'd always been with us, those two who stomped our streets, hunched and shrouded in black. They gave respective one-man shows on alternate nights, except Sunday. Growling Poe performed on Monday, Wednesday, and Friday; Smiling Poe on Tuesday, Thursday, and Saturday. Both performances were sparsely attended. In one famous instance, Growling Poe did a beseeching, raging version of his show for one deaf senior citizen who hadn't even come there for Poe. The woman had stumbled down into the dark catacombs on a far different mission. She was looking, she told the angry, pacing, furious-haired man, for her beloved kitty. Growling Poe was already irate that nobody had shown up that night and imagined that she'd been sent by his enemies to make a clown of him. He repeated her question in a diabolical whisper:

Have I seen your kitty? This confused the old woman, because she could read lips. "Yes, that's what I asked. Have you seen my cat? She likes to roam down here. This isn't the first time. Naughty pussy crawls in through a window."

And Growling Poe said it again, except this time it wasn't a question. "Have I seen your kitty! My dear, Muddy, I'm afraid I have. Something's happened."

"To Punim?"

"Yes, to Punim." He jabbed a finger toward a folding chair. "Sit." And as the old bird watched in terror, begging him to return Punim alive, Growling Poe launched into his second act, an abbreviated telling of "The Black Cat," cutting right to the moment when the pet assassin reaches down and gouges out the eye of the feline who torments him with love.

Although on the surface at least, Smiling Poe was a kinder man than Growling Poe—all the merchants downtown would tell you this—Smiling Poe didn't have much better luck luring people down to the catacombs for his shows. So why, you might ask, an Edgar Allan Poe Festival in our town when our idea of theater is the high school's annual abomination of *Li'l Abner*? It's a good question, but if you have to ask, you don't know Rita Larry-Pontewitz. Rita Larry-Pontewitz is famous for being a thrice-widowed eccentric with incurable boredom and more money than our town's two savings-and-loans can handle. She likes to pretend that we care more about culture than we actually do. Thus, every few years or so she pours a little of her fortune into a project designed to bring us culture and tourist revenue. "Gonna put us on the map," she shouts, as she cruises down our sidewalks in her golf cart, handing out flyers for the ballet, the opera, ancient Chinese table dancing. She's never asked us if we wanted anybody to find us or not, but we tolerate her because she often donates money for things we do need, like a new monorail system connecting our old mall with our new mall and the reconstructed driving range and put-put center we named in her honor.

In the beginning, we were even excited about the festival and hauled out our forgotten copies of Poe from cardboard boxes in the attic and stayed up nights rereading "The Masque of the Red Death," "The Oblong Box," "Hop-Frog," and "The Murders in the Rue Morgue," after which we were again surprised and mildly annoyed that those killings were all an innocent monkey's havoc. We dutifully attended the art exhibitions and the Vincent Price movies, and we happily bought tickets for the one-man shows given in the basement of our Historical Society, which the society president and chief tour guide, Hal Hodapp, renamed the catacombs. The catacombs were a dank, cramped basement filled with stacks of molding telephone books that made people sneeze so loudly and profusely during performances you sometimes couldn't hear either Poe. But Hal Hodapp, who serves also as Rita Larry-Pontewitz's unofficial propagandist, circulated the story that the basement of the Historical Society had been an execution chamber back when beheading was still legal in our county. So the catacombs it was, no matter how much mold, and Hal, who shared Rita's desire to put us on the map, placed signs along the I-73 corridor to attract tourists to the festival. SEE NOT ONE BUT TWO EDGAR A. POES IN CHAMBER OF LOST HEADS.

Most people in town saw both Growling Poe's and Smiling Poe's show at least once. All well and good. We clapped and clapped. That was that. It was time for everyone to go back to the Betamax and boccie ball. Our literary interlude was over. We tromped our books back down to the basement, because they crowded our shelves. Then an odd thing. They didn't leave. Even after the rest of the festival packed it up and moved on to Kenosha. Even after Rita herself lost all interest in Edgar Allan Poe and disparaged him and his impersonators in the streets, a mother casting stones at her babies. "All right, enough already!" she yowled from her golf cart. "Besides, the real one was a drunk and married his eight-year-old sister! Is this the kind of role model we want to encourage for today's lusty youth?" She'd already begun to plan her next project, a tribute to our town's glassblowing heritage. To his credit—though he began to do Rita's bidding by inventing a glassblowing heritage, complete with an archaeological dig behind Kroger's—Hal Hodapp stuck with the Poes and didn't, despite Rita's thunder, evict them from the catacombs. Hal maintained that their voices kept the rats from coming upstairs and gnawing the carpet.

Neither Poe ever spoke to the other. We assumed, without giving it much thought, that the nature of being Poe is such that there can't be more than one of you. Why they both decided to stay is anyone's guess, but I'd say the two Poes agreed on one thing: that art need not be seen by human eyes to be art, even when it's drama. Still, it was funny to see two identically dressed men in period clothes pass each other on the street without a word, Growling Poe glaring, Smiling Poe raising the corners of his mouth—slightly—but enough for us to notice and remark that the more he smiled, the worse he looked.

They kept at it, week after week, month after month, depending on handfuls of tourists. Hal told us that in February there was no audience for either show for two weeks running. But every weeknight and Saturday they went on anyway, performing entire shows for rows of empty folding chairs. Hal knew because he lived upstairs at the Historical Society and admitted, when Rita Larry-Pontewitz wasn't around, that he liked to listen to the Poes from the open door of an old laundry chute.

At this point, I should confess, though I am no one important, that I felt there was something not quite right about Smiling Poe. He had, if this is possible, too much talent for his work. For me, Growling Poe was easier. He was a simple, vengeful man and therefore consistent. His openly hostile demeanor when he walked our streets matched his stage presence. His show was mostly shouted fury. Growling Poe's Poe anticipated that the world would turn against him—and the world delivered as promised. When I saw Growling Poe's show, I was depressed, anxious, pessimistic, but never *afraid*. I didn't fear death to the degree of a constant squeezing pressure against the temples. Growling Poe didn't overcome me with dread. But isn't dread what we ask of a Poe? I, who have never had anybody to lose and am still waiting, know that even Growling Poe's delivery of "The Raven" was complacent. It was as if he'd always expected to lose Lenore. Growling Poe reveled in the easy and dismal; what could this misery known as life bring you other than the loss of love? And so, he enjoyed his own anger too much to feel a single word of the poem he had memorized, acted so beautifully. He missed the point. Wasn't it Emerson who said that every single word is a poem? If anyone ever has, the real Poe understood this too well, as his hand stiffened and he could no longer hold his pen to write even one more of Emerson's sacred words in that cold house of his. And you know damn well that he couldn't reach for his wife's precious little hand, because she, young thing, was as cold as he was, and after that she was dying, and the dying have no warmth to give the living. Forgive me for getting carried away. Because we know all this, don't we? We've heard it all before. We die alone, and the real Poe wrote this out in his own blood, and though Growling Poe had done all his homework (in his program notes he wrote that he'd read all the books in Roderick Usher's library, including, of course, the *Directorium Inquisitorium* by the Dominican Eymeric de Gironne), he never understood how quickly our anger at being left dissolves into a loneliness no words can describe, not even words on the page. You can't take hold of the powdered hands of the dead, and this is what Smiling Poe understood too well. Embedded in his quiet smile was always the aloneness of grasping for a hand that's gone.

He was a short, bulbous man, much smaller than Growling Poe, with a missing front tooth. When he spoke, his voice whistled out in a soft hiss. He had the accent of a distant place which we couldn't, even with an atlas, identify. Somebody said he must be from Missouri, but somebody with an Aunt Leona in St. Louis insisted that if he was from anywhere, he was from south of Cape Girardeau. We never asked him directly. None of us ever spoke to either Poe, and Smiling Poe was even more unapproachable than Growling Poe, who, though he spoke harshly to our grocers, florists, and stationers, at least made pretense of conversation. For instance, Growling Poe would say things like: "Do you always sell rotting vegetables?" or "Is there a particular day of the week you don't cheat people?" Smiling Poe, on the other hand, always spoke politely, but always at, never *to*. He was the one who scared us, and although his show was slow in spots, especially during his ten-minute attack on that vapid Professor Longfellow, the horror of emptiness, the sadness of the tomb, lurked in every word he softly uttered. During "The Cask of Amontillado" you could hear drunken Fortunato's groans for mercy as if they were pleading from your own chest. It wasn't pleasant, Smiling Poe's show, but it was necessary. Yet, twice was enough dread, even for me. Who wants to be reminded more than that that we're all Fortunato? That we'll all, every one of us, beg the joke over as the mason walls us in?

The fact of his being still down there began to grate—and it went beyond my nerves. Other people had the same notions, but nobody dared talk about it. You didn't need to see his show more than once to feel his presence all over town. Tuesday, Thursday, and Saturday, that same death drifting up out of the basement. Monday, Wednesday, Friday were an imitation—this we could tolerate. We started ignoring Smiling Poe harder. When we saw him haunting the sidewalks, we ducked into insurance agents' offices or the dry cleaners to avoid seeing his face and that missing tooth. Growling Poe got blithery about parking tickets and bad vegetables and bird shit on the hood of his rented Toyota and, though not a stellar actor, was at least *human*. Smiling Poe walked above us with that grin that jutted from his lips like a knife blade, and after thirty weeks of it we began to sympathize with Rita Larry-Pontewitz's campaign to ban the genuine Poe from the library and his impersonators from our city limits. Growling Poe, too, if only because his clothes and big forehead reminded us too much of Smiling Poe.

And still they gave shows—ticket prices had long since

been slashed in half—always to unsuspecting tourists hungering for a bargain (who cared what it was?) who'd been lured to town by Rita and Hal, who had put us on the map. We were starting to become known as the town that couldn't get rid of its Poes. Until. Isn't there always an "until" in stories of death? And what story is not, finally, about death?

It happened on a Tuesday night during Smiling Poe's show. It was almost spring, and after a long winter, tourist attendance for the shows had actually been picking up. That night Hal Hodapp, who was handing out flyers in the Historical Society foyer advertising our glassblowing exhibition, had counted five people descending into the catacombs when he noticed that one of them was Growling Poe in disguise. Hal said it wasn't a very good disguise, but different enough for him that he looked like a new man. He was dressed like an average guy about our town, his hair combed forward, wearing a faded Izod shirt, circa 1972. Hal was curious, because to his knowledge neither Poe had ever seen the other's show, so he followed the short line downstairs. He told us later at the Blue Parrot that it was a virtuoso performance, the best he'd ever seen in person or listened to from the laundry chute. That Smiling Poe looked like he'd lost weight, that his face had begun to shrivel, raisin-like, and his one front tooth gleamed a hideous yellow in the shallow light. Two cats rubbed against his legs, and what was so terrible, Hal said, was that Smiling Poe acted kindly toward the cats, that often in the middle of the show he reached down with his skull-colored hands and rubbed them. Hal said all he wanted was to leave and go upstairs and curl up with his electric blanket turned all the way to twelve, because Smiling Poe emanated cold, even as his hand stroked the cats. But he had stayed because he wanted to watch Growling Poe's reactions. And at our table at the Blue Parrot, Hal said Growling Poe's face during the show reminded him of the men he'd imagined about to be beheaded in that very room. Because his eyes never moved, never twitched.

Nobody will ever know if he planned it in advance or if it came to him in a sudden jolt of jealous inspiration, but during Smiling Poe's almost entirely whispered "Raven," Growling Poe threw his voice at the very moment of the bird's first "Nevermore." Growling Poe was as mediocre a ventriloquist as he was an actor, Hal said, but it was good enough, and Smiling Poe looked up at the corner to the left of the papier-mâché bust of Pallus, and he didn't stop, didn't say, "Nevermore," just went on with the poem. Each time it was the bird's turn to talk, he let the corner do it. Hal said that by the third or fourth time, all four tourists from Schaumburg knew it was the guy in the third row, in the pale golf shirt, but by that time Smiling Poe believed in the voice.

Hal's eyes got red, and he thrust down the last of his 7-Up. "I tell you, the man thought he'd reached beyond the grave, that after thousands of "Ravens" he'd finally broken through to someone. To the devil, to God, to Poe himself, or—" Hal paused and we all leaned forward. I noticed Hal's gums had turned the color of ash. "Or, to his own Lenore."

When he reached the poem's final moment, Smiling Poe said so softly you had to strain to hear him, like a man swimming to the surface of a dream:

> *And my soul from out that shadow that lies*
> *   floating on the floor*
> *Shall be lifted—*

And he waited, as though he actually expected the dread word to come later than before. And he stood there smiling that awful smile, his legs akimbo.

Shall be lifted—

And still there was nothing from the corner.

"I didn't look at Growling Poe at that point," Hal said. "How could I? Man so cruel to lead another man into belief and then rip the rug out like it's nothing."

Smiling Poe didn't continue. Hal told us that after his unfinished "Raven," he just walked out, although there was a good fifteen minutes left and the Montresor still had to murder Fortunato. They listened to his slow clod up the stairs. Nobody moved. Everybody, even the cats, watched the corner. Hal said he even prayed. Then Hal backed up his chair, dropped three quarters on the table, and left us. We listened to one of the quarters bounce and spin before landing flat, and we felt ashamed, though we couldn't have said why. And even now, even years after, when shame still coats us like the fine dust we often wear, thanks to the cement factory north of town, we still can't say why.

They found him Wednesday morning drooping from a light fixture in his hotel room. There was an unfinished sandwich on the table and two black suits in the closet. The coroner said, medically speaking, Smiling Poe had been dead for at least eight hours, but the cleaning woman who found him swore—she still swears—that when she opened the door he was still writhing, that he didn't stop moving until she touched him, poor man, never seen anybody look so lonely— not dead, lonely.

Shoe Story

THE PHONE deadly silent, I recall a certain pair of shoes. We were at Ike's, at our table by the window, having burgers and sloppy cheese fries, and I was whining about Devon and how she'd dumped me for the twenty-seventh time. On my ass this time, I said. And this time, this time, I swear I won't call her back when she calls. This time I'm going to have R-E-S-O-L-V-E. This time when I say I'm going to do something, by fucking God, I'm going to do it. Cal yawned a long yawn. He'd heard it all before and didn't want to waste his breath on eloquence he'd already orated, as he put it. We were circling again. Ike's, burgers, cheese fries, Devon dumping me number 22, 23, 24, 25, 26 . . . But during take number 27 something happened, something that pushed us out of our routine. A woman's voice. Crass and loud and roaring and beautiful and low. A woman's voice, upstairs, in the apartment above Ike's.

Liar! Nobody lies like you! Nobody! You lie and you lie and you lie, and when you say you're not lying anymore, you lie about whether you're lying.

Bullshit, a man retorted. Meek, but not dead yet. Bullshit. What about Martin Jumbileau?

Martin Jumbileau? she raged. Martin Jumbileau! You mean you're going to bring him into this? Like I'm some kind of lowlife you pulled off the street and saved. Tanya's right. You are foul.

Then she winged her shoes at him.

I know this because Cal and I were sitting there listening, wiping our hands on our pants—Ike's got no napkins—when two white shoes dropped into the street like tiny planes crash-landing. Women's patent-leather pumps with straps. They lay sprawled on the pavement, toe to toe, linked in the agony of the fall.

Cal and I stared out the window at those snazzy shoes as we listened to the silence of victory unfold in the apartment upstairs. And the world was merciful. It did stop its spin, and those shoes were angels dispatched to rescue ourselves from our own grease-soaked and burbling-over hearts.

Thursday Night at the Gopher Hole, April 1992

ON A THURSDAY NIGHT, in the tiny men's room at the Gopher Hole in Gilbertsville, Iowa, in the infamous pisser with the hidden step down—ask Candice what happened to Frank Knipp's forehead when it met the urinal after he tripped in the dark—the other Frank, the quiet one, Frank Waverly, saw something alarming in the mirror. Odd furrows, just above and below his eyes, ruts that looked like they were somehow getting deeper by the moment. And his cheeks were now twin percolating spasms. Frank Waverly stared at himself. He'd had two, three beers; he wasn't drunk. Frank Waverly rarely got drunk. He was known as a light drinker who thought a lot about things, a methodical man who trolled around for answers before making judgments. For this reason, he was a man who could always be called upon to fix odd things—not because he was so clever with his hands, but because he studied what was wrong with something before he touched any of the parts.

Examining his face more closely, Frank went through some of the possible explanations for this strange turmoil. He knew immediately that whatever it was had nothing to do with fear of marriage, of having to be with Nancy forever even if things didn't pan out, or fear that sex wouldn't be any good after. All that crap that Raymond and Pauly Sicosh kept razzing him about. He wasn't afraid of weddings—it was the only thing he'd ever really wanted. When they were boys, his brother Lance drew pictures of himself as a dentist torturing babies; Frank's drawings were of tuxedos and veils and four-story cakes the size of the Kickapoo township landfill. So it wasn't Nancy. Nor was it her last name, which was enough to shrivel the balls of most men in town. You had to tread carefully when dealing with a Degardelle, particularly a female Degardelle. If something went wrong, you'd end up with a posse of mothers and aunts and eighteenth cousins chasing you to Sioux City with shovels and rakes and firearms. Nobody (and this had been true, people said, since the Civil War) embarrassed that family and got away with it. Chick Larson's stunt with Nancy's cousin Theresa was an obvious case in point. His famous two-days-before-the-wedding waffle; now he lives under Buicks at the Jiffy Lube in Cedar Falls. But Frank had gone to school with Degardelles (Randall, Stevo, Little Joey). He'd delivered pizzas with Degardelles (Little Joey, Chubby Marcy). He'd been surrounded his whole life by that locally royal family. He wasn't intimidated by them and besides—and on this he truly walked alone—he actually liked Nancy's mother. Not accepted, feared, or stood in awe of, but liked. She had been his third-grade teacher (now she was Superintendent of Schools), and even though she'd stomped on his foot whenever he stuttered his T's, she'd taught him to read.

The bizarre doings in his face didn't stop. His gurgling cheeks were beginning to expand. He thought of Nancy after she got her wisdom teeth pulled and came home morphed into Louis Armstrong. And it wasn't that Nancy talked too much, even though she did. That was what he loved about her, that she never stopped the chatter, that she went on about who knew what half the time. Babbling onward about Nick Desmond's wife, Suzie, and how nuts she was with her backward jogging. Then she'd switch and talk about summers up at the Degardelle family cottage in Rhinelander. Then, a related story, maybe, about her Uncle Vasco and his seasonal pedophilia. Then she'd inexplicably about-face into another merciless attack on Barbra Streisand. "I mean what the hell do I care how many neuroses she has?" What mattered to Frank was not the content but the dependability of her patter. Nancy filled the often unendurable silences of his life. He didn't exist in silence literally. S and F Packaging was as loud a place as any. It was just that there were times in the day—even when he was working side by side with people—when he'd feel the silence build to a low whine, as if a mosquito were trapped and slowly dying in his ear. An odd, sometimes nagging, sometimes blissful silence that cut him off from everybody, even his closest friends, guys he'd grown up with and now worked beside. Guys whose kids called him the Other Uncle Frank on the Fourth of July. For the most part he hid the problem well. Nobody except Nancy even knew about it. Whenever it was obvious to others that Frank was trying to read their lips rather than listen to them, most just thought, That's Frank Waverly, thinking so hard about other things that he can't keep up.

For a long time he'd been certain that his brother was the cause of what he considered his private condition. He might be filling an invoice code or on hold with a wholesaler when he'd be struck by the simple thudding fact of his brother.

That his brother hiccuped, that his brother farted, that he could do both, proudly, at the same time. That it was Lance who once changed the channel for an entire hour. That Lance was the one who squirted his mother's hair jizz in both his ears and asked him if he could hear the Pacific Ocean now. That he was the one who cross-country skied on the roof of Hoover Elementary and whooped at the fat cop to come up and get him if it was so illegal. That it was Lance who threw the alarm clock and then the basketball to wake him up on the morning of a day he has no other reason to remember now. Sometimes he thinks he's co-opted his brother's dumbest memories and made them his own, because remembering what Lance did is easier than remembering the physical Lance, the one with the disgusting fungus toes, the one who slept with his eyes half open, like a bad imitation of a dead guy.

Frank gripped the sides of the sink and glared at himself in the murky light. Someone jiggled the door handle. Frank's shoulders knotted, the way they did if anyone tapped him from behind when he was in the silence. Except now he was watching it happen in the mirror, and it wasn't temporary. His shoulders stayed hunched. The ruts around his eyes were deepening into ditches and his cheeks were still blimping. A dark-purple fluid was beginning to drip from his nose into the sink. The handle rattled again. Frank managed a shallow "Still in here." Whoever it was—it sounded like Tony Lemoyne—said, "Laying an egg in there or what?" Frank didn't answer. He just kept staring. Not only at everything that was going wrong in his face, but also at the things that remained the same. His skimpy eyebrows, his slightly bucked teeth, his disproportionately fat upper lip. At the mustache he'd hated for six months but didn't shave off and couldn't say why not.

He pressed the tab of the soap dispenser and caught the pink splat. He foamed up his face and rinsed, but still couldn't get rid of any of it, what was new or what was him. He checked his pulse, which seemed okay, though the Red Cross class had been years ago and he couldn't remember how long to keep his fingers on his wrist. But there was a beat there. One, one, one, one, one. Then he said, out loud, "God?" It was unlike Frank in that he didn't think about it before he blurted. It came from his mouth not his brain. Here in this bathroom that Candice cleans twice a year, once because she always hides Easter eggs behind the toilet and again before the health inspector comes. That asshole Lemoyne kicked the door. "There's a man out here that's gonna start squealing like a pig." Frank laughed, but not at Lemoyne. No one laughed at Lemoyne, even when he was funny. Nancy once asked him if he was an atheist. Her Grandmother Degardelle was worried. He'd lied, said he was a believer. Now here he is, a secret blasphemer, in this stink of a bathroom with Tony Lemoyne holding his legs together outside the door, trying to read his face for a message from on high. Shit, if John Denver can talk to Him in the rearview mirror of a Pinto, why not me? He hoped it didn't have anything to do with politics, because he hadn't read the *Register* in days. Maybe this has something to do with Sadaam again. Another call to arms. Rallying the troops to kill some more Arabs in the name of the Father, the Son, and the Holy Ghost. If that was the case, though, why wouldn't He go through Raymond, because he'd been in Desert Storm the first time around and he was right there at the bar? (Or Nancy, because she videotapes C-Span.) Frank's eyes turned from their usual hazy brown to black, and his upper lip curled over his mustache and began to dam up the purple fluid, so that he started to breathe it back up his nose. He finally got scared and considered leaving his face and calling Nancy—Candice would let him use the phone behind the bar. He would tell her what was happening, and Nancy would say, Wow, Frank, reminds me of that Bible thumper convention my sister Julia dragged me to: eighty thousand people in a football stadium taking turns narrating their personal experiences with God. God on the call-waiting, God on the intercom at the Department of Motor Vehicles, God in the plastic-only recyclables. What'd you say was wrong with your nose, Frank? Disgusting purple what's coming out of your nostrils?

Talk about embarrassing Degardelles if he walked out of there looking like this. He thought of what Lance would say if he could see him now. *You know the real miracle here, Frank, is that you haven't gotten all that uglier.* And it was then that he prayed, for the first time, without watching himself and laughing. Prayed that his brother, though he loved to inflict pain, had felt none. Frank prayed standing, still gripping the sink, still watching the siege in his face. Lance changing a tire too close to the road and the trucker, who maybe dozed for a split second or maybe didn't see him, edged a sliver to the right and, without even nicking the Impala, ended Lance at seventeen. He prayed for Lance and the trucker who'd scooped him up and brought the bloody mass that was his brother to the emergency room. When the trucker heard that Lance was gone, he'd stormed out of the hospital and dumped his cargo into the parking lot, kicking and dragging boxes, ranting, *How late, Mr. Haskins? How fucking late am I now, Mr. Keith Haskins?* He went on for hours, whacking away at boxes and cursing Haskins. His mother always insisted that the trucker's performance in the parking lot was grief over himself, over the potential loss of his job, his license, his reputation. She said she forgave him, but that didn't mean she had to believe him. I'm sorry to say it, she said, but nobody gets that crazy over a stranger. But Frank had an idea then—and he was only twelve when all this happened—that his mother was a fool. And here was that trucker now staring out from his own bloated face, his own raging face, still furious, still shouting—on his way somewhere then, now going nowhere, still in the parking lot hysterical.

Lemoyne kicked the door harder. Some other guys joined him. He heard Candice say, Maybe he knocked himself out like Frank Knipp did that time. What's with the Franks? Maybe they should start pissing in the alley behind Daskell's. And he heard Raymond shout: "You defrosting the tenderloin in there, Frank?" Somebody—it sounded like Cash Lorimer—asked why Candice didn't just go and get the key, and Candice screamed, It bolts from the inside, dildo! Frank pinched the bulb of his oozing nose and tried to hold his breath. Raymond had once told him that there's no real difference between faith and endurance. He talked about the waiting and the hoping after he got back from the Gulf, even though he'd confessed in a whisper to Frank that working the computer on the USS *Saratoga* was about as dangerous as dealing blackjack on the gambling boat in Bentendorf. "Even had women commanders in tight pants. Not like my Uncle Telly getting his ass cheeks shot off at Chui Lai." He thought of Nancy's fearless gobble-gobble. How there was always the chance she'd circle around to a point. So he continued to watch himself as the old familiar silence engulfed his ears and the racket they were making outside the door became low and faintly melodious, and then it got so soft he couldn't hear it anymore, like the moment just after a song fades for good but somehow it's still there. And even later, when their pounding drifted as far away as his brother, he recalled the shouts, their concern, their alarm, with fondness.

County Road G

H ER NAME was Clare Warnoc and she was from Superior, Wisconsin, and she was out in the country on her
way to visit her sister in Solan Springs. His name—it came
out later—was Frank Troyer, of Frank Troyer Trucking, Ashland. The discovery happened roughly like this: Clare, whose
vision had always been better than her sister's (Clare told her
bridge friends back in Superior that Evelyn wouldn't have noticed the murdered man if he had dropped out of the sky and
crashed into the hood of her Fairmont), was driving west on
County Road G, past Score's Bait, past the Norwood Golf
and Driving Range, when, just before the north entrance to
the Nekoosa Industrial Forest, she spotted, through a stand
of bare poplars, a pair of blue-jeaned legs and booted feet
hanging out of what even from that distance she could see
was a bathtub. Clare said she saw the whole picture all at
once like that. She said it was one of those rare times when
your first view of something from a ways away is right on target. She pulled over, and a closer look verified it: a dead man
in a discarded tub. Then Clare, who, unlike her sister Evelyn,
had never waited out a shy moment in her life, immediately
reached down into the thick green murk of a three-nights-

ago rain and yanked up the man's wrist. Dead and slimy as a trout in a plastic bag. After that Clare stood for a couple of moments and examined the dead man's face before walking without hurry back to her car. When she arrived at Evelyn's, Clare called the Douglas County sheriff, a man named Furf, a man with an aching back and sweaty feet, a man who at first didn't believe her story.

The circumstances of the murder were reported in the Duluth *Herald-Tribune,* the *Superior Telegraph,* and the local Spooner paper. The crime was categorized in the police report as domestic in nature. Frank Troyer was involved with someone else's wife. Her name was Carrie Somskins. The husband was a hothead named Richard. They lived in Hayward, but Carrie had gone to high school with Troyer back in the late seventies. They'd gone to the junior prom together. In April 1988, Carrie and Troyer bumped into each other at the pumps at the Holiday Station in Iron River. They had both been struggling for a while. Carrie's marriage had never been happy; Troyer was already divorced. It didn't take a lot to rekindle the high school flames. One thing led to another, and before either of them could catch a breath, the thing was full-blown. Then came crazy talk of Carrie filing for divorce and them moving to the Twin Cities, starting over. They were never serious about it, but that didn't keep them from talking their dreams. And writing them. One of Carrie's kids, while raiding his mother's purse for Tic Tacs, found a letter Troyer had written to Carrie. The boy was loyal to his father.

No one has been able to explain why Richard Somskins stuffed Frank Troyer's body in an abandoned bathtub only seventeen miles from his house, although more than a few people in Spooner and Hayward and Solan Springs speculated at the time that it had a lot to do with the contents of that letter, which was never found. Richard went mute after his arrest. Refused to say a word to his lawyers, the cops, anybody. That made the papers, too. The "dumbstruck killer" is what they called him in the *Telegraph*. In court, he just sat there slack-faced and refused to speak to the judge or even enter a plea. His lawyer tried to have him declared insane, but there was no law that said you were nuts if you didn't talk. When Carrie brought the kids to the county jail in Ashland on the eve of his conviction, he smiled at each of them—including Carrie—but still refused to say even a single word.

There's this also. Four years after she discovered Frank Troyer's body, on December 20, 1994, Clare Warnoc spent the last ten minutes of her conscious life talking to a nurse named Meryl Dudziak at Superior Memorial Hospital. Clare told Meryl something she had never told her bridge friends, or even Evelyn, who had passed on in '92. She told Meryl about Frank Troyer's face, how it was sticking out of the water so that she could see his eyes and nose. Frank Troyer's face, purple and fat-cheeked, but kind-looking, too. She could see that for certain. And her instincts were right. People said at the time (and the local Spooner paper reported) that Frank Troyer was known for never being serious, and so, considered always dependable. Never got excited. He'd never turn you down is what a lot of people said. The man would laugh if you asked him to haul scrap at the last minute, laugh because you bothered to ask, as if it would be any trouble . . . Clare Warnoc told Meryl Dudziak that for a moment she mistook the corpse's bloated face for her brother Jed's. Jed, who was killed in the war, dead at twenty-five, fighting Mussolini in Africa. Jed with his stupid jokes and his wild, hairy, pinching fingers. Jed whom she hadn't laid eyes on since 1943. Jed, who kissed her and swapped her on the head with his flimsy hat. Clare gripped Meryl's thin wrist and told her that out on that road, in front of that tub, she thought she'd found her brother. I've never been a woman to fantasize or make up stories. You probably know that about me already, Meryl dear. But my heart got crushed out there on that road, because for a half a second I wanted to shake him and scream, *All these years, Jeddy. All these years.*

At the Motel Rainbow

SET BACK beyond the highway trees, the ruins of the Motel Rainbow five miles west of Iron River, Wisconsin. In its day a perfectly respectable place to stop and sleep for the night, but now long abandoned. Since '91, when the owners, Duane and Theresa Fjelstad, split up for good and the mortgage stopped getting paid. Neither of them wanted or could afford to run the place alone, and they couldn't live together anymore. Fourteen years and poof, and few people even noticed the Rainbow was no longer, except for a couple of fishermen from Escanaba who'd made a ritual of staying there during the week they fished the Brule. The two of them had camped out in the parking lot the year they found their favorite motel closed. The state bank in Hayward has sat on the land ever since, waiting it out for some white-knight developer with plans for a minimart. Or better yet, for a casino-happy tribe with state authorization to construct a warehouse of slot machines like the one in Black River.

But for now the place remains. One long, narrow, red brick building, with the old manager's office in the middle painted yellow. A wooden sign with a rainbow out front. A broken neon NO VACANCY/VACANCY light under it. Out of one window hangs the remains of a curtain, twisted like a girl's braid. And by the road a wind-mangled cardboard FOR SALE sign leaning crookedly out of the ground. The place is mostly boarded up, but somebody did a poor job of it and there are a few gaps, entry points. Local kids from Chetek High School climb through the exposed broken windows and smoke dope and drink in the old rooms. Although most of the rooms are empty now, there is one room—12C—that still has a ratty mattress and a broken television.

Wade brought his own sheets from home. They didn't fit— the mattress was a queen—but Sue wrapped herself up in them to avoid touching the mattress with her skin and laughed, saying he could at least have taken her to a place that wasn't condemned. Then she kissed him and told him that she didn't care, that she'd never care, and that she'd always remember this place like it was the new Ramada in Duluth. Wade was proud of himself, proud that he'd remembered to bring everything. (Sue always busted his balls because he forgot his wallet that time he took her to the Chinese place in Washburn.) Condoms, beer, blankets, sheets, tape player, flashlight, C batteries, double A's, a magazine so that if Sue got bored he could read to her. They didn't wait very long. They were both so excited, they went right ahead with it—Wade on top, and the two of them gripping each other's shoulders as if the other was the seat in front on a crashing plane. It was over quicker than either of them had dreamed, especially Sue, but it was great, and actually different from everything else. And after, Sue squeezed her legs around him and nibbled his chin and told him she loved him a lot and how weird that was considering he was such a complete flake. Wade, who'd forgotten to turn on the music before they started, reached to the floor and found the Play button. The tape was a mix he'd made for the occasion, with Frampton's "Baby, I Love Your Way" and mellow U2. It was around 9:45 and finally getting dark. This was a Tuesday in the middle of July. Tuesday night, the night Wade had scoped out, the night nobody ever went over to hang out at the Rainbow.

Wade hadn't thought of bringing a candle, so he stood up and tied the flashlight (using the rubber strap attachment) to a rusty fixture above the bed. The whole time he was fiddling, Sue kept leaping up and kissing his stomach, tugging at the little hairs above his belly button with her front teeth. When he had the light rigged up, he pushed it so that it circled, the beam exposing the room. One of the two big windows was boarded up, as was the door. The other big window was kicked out (that's how they'd got in), and the small window above the door was also broken. That one probably by a rock, just for the hell of it; the hole in the glass was jagged, star-shaped. The TV was ancient, a big Zenith built into a large wooden case, a throwback to the time when TVs were more like furniture. The knobs were ripped off, and somebody had spray-painted SUCK across the screen. They were sixteen and they had their own room and the flashlight twirled above them. Wade held Sue's elbows. They squinted at each other, both their expressions a combination of pride, fear, and embarrassment at the line they'd crossed, because now even just walking around the halls at school would be different. Everybody said it was no big deal, and everybody lied, and though they both knew there was no reason to look back at those virgin days, there was equally no point in not reveling in this moment. So they lingered in the fact of sex. The walking around school would come later. They would learn that swagger soon enough.

"Are you going to tell Marcy?" Wade asked.

Sue clucked her tongue. "You want me not to?" The flashlight above their heads stopped circling and now pointed straight down at them like a small spotlight.

"I just wanted to know."

"No. Not for a while at least. She's a total mouth."

Wade squeezed her elbows tighter. Giddiness kicked up his heartbeat. Everybody knowing. He didn't say anything.

"My stepdad thinks you're a fuck-up and you probably won't go to college," Sue said.

"Tell him next time I feel like mixing paint at Poplar Hardware for the rest of my life, I'll give him a call."

"Okay," Sue said, and kissed his ear. "I'll tell him, peanut. And he'll tell me he's one-third owner of Poplar Hardware, *a True Value subsidiary,* and then he'll say my little boyfriend's afraid of real work."

"Tell him I'm going to college in California and then I'm going to drop out and just drive."

"Drive to Mexico, drive to Russia. Drive to damn Hawaii. You think you can drive everywhere and gas money's going to flow out the glove compartment like a cash machine."

"You want to come with?"

"To Hawaii, yes. And to Jamaica, maybe." Sue paused and looked at him straight on. "Wade, this place doesn't even have a toilet."

Wade undid the flashlight, and they both pulled on underwear and shoes and stepped out through the window. The temperature had dropped into the sixties, and Wade felt a little wind on his arms. The moon glowed behind the clouds; the night was pale and starless. Sue walked over to the pines and squatted. Wade pointed the light at her. "Don't be an asshole," she said, and he swung the light at the row of dead rooms and the yellow boarded-up manager's office in the middle. Then he walked around the side to check on his car and to take a piss himself. The car was tucked into the trees where he'd left it. He rubbed his trunk. Also back there was an old swimming pool. As he pissed, Wade looked at the hole in the ground and the flimsy and trampled plastic fence that surrounded it. Old danger signs in the mud. He thought of people actually splashing around in that pool, and now look at it. An eyesore, dirty rainwater at the bottom. A couple of times Wade and his friends went to the empty pool to skateboard, that year he skateboarded. He touched his car again before walking back around front. Sue met him in the parking lot. "Next time let's go real camping, or at least to a place with a real bathroom, like a Yogi Bear. My dad used to take us to a Yogi Bear. The one near Minong. God, did that place suck, but at least it had bathrooms. We could go to a campground next time, Wade."

"I thought you liked this place—Watch!" Wade turned the flashlight on his own face and shook it hard, moved his head a little. His face blanched and eerie in the handmade strobe.

"Cut it out."

"But you said before you liked this place. That you'd always remember it."

"I didn't say I liked it, Wade. I said I'd remember it. I'll remember that it was a little strange."

"But it's ours," he said, and he locked his arms around her hips and started walking backward across the gravel, pulling her with him. Sue was taller, so he walked on tiptoe and lodged his chin in the scoop of her shoulder as he steered them back to the room.

Wade rerigged the flashlight, and they talked some more about Marcy. Sue said she screwed around with Kenny Heetz and Avy Thompson on the same night. She told him that Cindy Balter got another DUI. "They're going to take her license away, and I say good. She deserves it. She's already hit two deer this summer." And they talked about work—they were both lifeguards at Lake Hulbert Beach—and how it was so boring because there was never anybody to save.

"I mean I'd save a dog," Sue said.

They'd both been sitting in the sun all day. That and the excitement of going ahead and doing what they'd been whispering about since April made them both fall asleep just after eleven.

An hour later Wade woke up in the drainy low-battery light. Sue didn't move when Wade stood up to flick off the flashlight. He nuzzled closer to her in the now darker but now somehow more familiar room. A shadowy little hideout, like the old fort behind Jay Nichols's father's place. That fort was really an old shed swallowed by weeds. He and Jay had painted LOYAL ORDER OF THE ODDFELLOWS #561 in black on the door. Wade had always loved abandoned places more than where people lived. Those collapsed barns along County B between Brule and Lake Nebagamon. The burned-out factories in Superior at the end of Tower Avenue, where the strip clubs are.

Once in Ino, right off 53 heading to Washburn/Bayfield, Wade found a crumbling boarded-up house with a piano. It was just sitting there in the middle of the front room, balanced on supports, because someone had bothered to rip out the floorboards but they didn't take the old piano. He'd stood there and doodled "Twinkle Twinkle Little Star" on the corroding keys for a while, thinking about all the long-gone fingers that had once touched them. This abandoned motel room was like that house with the piano, a place you could have as yours while you were there, and not because you'd paid somebody for it. Just like those woods behind Jay Nichols's father's place, or even the lake—the real lake, Superior, not Hulbert—because it's nobody's and everybody's. There for the taking if you've got the balls and can forget about money once in a while. So he'd taken this room—12C —and here they were. Jesus, Jay Nichols has been gone three years. His mother moved to South Carolina and took Jay with her. Better jobs down there. Or *were* better jobs. They'd missed whatever boom there was. The eighties are dead and buried, Wade's father had said, even though there was still a year to go when they left in '89. Wade's father was suspicious of anyone who left northern Wisconsin. He said Jay's mother had to be running from something, because this place is as good as any other place in the country, only colder sometimes . . . Christ, Wade thought, anybody else, like Avy Thompson, that chronic gloater, would have done it outside, on the beach at Anakoosh Point, or at the mouth of the Brule. But out there you risked a fisherman or an old woman waddling by in the morning and the whole moment ruined. Here they could sleep and wake up in the morning when they wanted. Sure, some of the hideousness of the place would shout at their morning eyes, but who would care? They'd done it. A Tuesday night melting into a summer Wednesday. Neither of them had to work till 12:30.

After, she said it was just a joke. At first that's what she said. After he'd marched barefoot the five miles back to Iron River and found his car parked on South Cotter Road around the corner from Sue's parents' place. After he'd pounded the front door, then the side, then the back. All locked. After he chucked a rock at her curtained window and shattered the pane and shouted. She peered out the broken window and looked down at her Wade and his fuming tomato face and said, "It was a joke, Wade." And she laughed at him. Then she went downstairs and opened the door and told him something closer to truth: "I drove away, Wade. Just like you're always talking about driving away."

She stood at the door in shorts, and he wanted to hit her. You fucking bitch. But he didn't say anything, just looked her over. At Sue, with her shorts and bare legs and applesauce yellow-brown hair and headphones on her neck and puggly nose and little sucked-in cheeks like two tiny waterless ponds.

"I thought you were kidnapped, raped. Jesus."

"Just drove away, Wade." Now not smiling, now glaring him straight in the face, so it felt as if he was the one being hit. "Just like you're always blabbing about doing."

He felt for her across the bed. Nothing. He opened his groggy eyes. Early, not much after seven, but the sun was hot already. Sweating. Alone in the bed. First, he figured she'd gone outside to the bathroom. But when he got up and looked out the window at the trees, he didn't see her. He shouted for her. No answer. He shouted again and listened, and all he heard was his own sudden panting. He slid his legs into his pants and climbed out the big window. He ran without shoes across the gravel to the stand of pines, knowing she wasn't there, because he could see she wasn't there, but checking anyway. Knowing she wasn't the type of person to take a walk on her own in the morning, and where the hell was there to walk to but the thick mosquitoed woods. Still trying to stay calm. Shouting calmly: *Sue! Suzy!* Nothing. Then screeching: *Suzy! Suzy!* He ran around the back and for some reason first looked in the empty pool and thought, Whatever the explanation for this, not waking up with her is the worst thing that will ever happen to me. He thought of his father dying. Thought of himself alone in the house, listening to the clocks. *I'm a disgrace as a son.* Ashamed but still knowing, even so, that this will always be worse, wherever Sue is, whatever happened, this right now will always be worse than any funeral. He ran on and arrived at the empty space where he'd hidden his car twelve hours earlier and felt in his pocket for his keys. And then—and this he knew with as much certainty as he knew that he'd be buried next to his father behind St. Bartholomew's—that there would be worse things than even this, so many worse things than this. He knelt down and touched the tire tracks in the mud as if their familiar pattern alone could explain why she'd done it.

Sue peeled out the gravel driveway and thought how kickass it felt to no longer be a virgin and speeding away in your boyfriend's car. It had everything to do with driving and leaving. But there was more. She loved him. She'd told him that.

He'd never told her, but that wasn't why she stole his keys and took off in his car at dawn. He didn't have to tell her. She knew he did. That wasn't it. And she didn't drive away because he was going to drive away from her sooner or later either. No. She realized as she drove down 53 and away from him and his gaped, sleeping mouth that she was driving away because he thought, One day I'm going to drive away. Because he aspired without her. Like he had some kind of birthright. Her father had gotten away with it. So as she sped by the Ino bar, things made more sense. She was punishing Wade's thinking. Not the real leaving. The real leaving—if he even had the guts, which was an open question—she could handle, just like her mother had, and maybe by then she wouldn't even care.

But then her driving became something more, and she drove west, away from Iron River, loving the car and the new blacktop on the two-lane to Poplar. No one on the road that early except for a few trucks. The tall pines of the Brule River State Forest on both sides, towering over the highway. Trees that meant home. The muddy trails that wound through them. The thousand deer. She kept going west and drove all the way to Route B, which circled around Lake Nebagamon, that quiet lake where she and Wade went once in a while to get away from Hulbert. The little beach with the raft. NO LIFEGUARD ON DUTY, SWIM AT YOUR OWN RISK. A sign they liked. They always did their best to lie on the beach and avoid watching the children splashing—refused to tell any of them not to push each other off the raft. She drove with her head out the window, wind gusting in her face, sometimes seeing glimpses of the lake through the damp green trees, sometimes not. Near the bait shop she got out and walked to the end of the dock and dangled her feet in the waveless water. A man was swimming across the small cove by the bridge, and she watched his slowly arcing arms. She thought of Wade stomping down the highway and his anger and how he wasn't going to get it and how she was going to have to explain it to him. When she got home, her mother and stepfather were both already at work. A note from her mother was waiting for her on the kitchen table pad. Her mother's looping, forgiving handwriting. She didn't read it.

Sitting Theodore

M RS. GOLD down the block in the colossal brick house tried to off her husband, a huge Cadillac-driving guy named Jerry, by hiring two hit men from Bollingbrook to murder him in the shower. Turned out one of the guys was an undercover Chicago cop specializing in domestic homicide. Later, in prison, Mrs. Gold fell in love with the lawyer working on her appeal, my mom's friend, the formerly unassuming and mousy Fran Swanner. This all happened in Morton Grove, Illinois, in 1981. There's more. When they sent her down to Five Hills Correctional in Centralia, Mrs. Gold was pregnant with the baby of one of the hit men, the real hit man, the one who wasn't a cop. Mrs. Gold was sentenced to six years, and for the first two, the baby, Theodore, lived with his mother at Five Hills. Then, on his second birthday, he moved into Fran Swanner's house on Cedar Valley Road. When Mrs. Gold got paroled a year later, she joined them.

Of course if only it had been that easy. Fran Swanner was married when she and Mrs. Gold fell hard for each other. To a courtly real estate agent named Don, and they had two very bright kids, twins. I think Jeremy ended up at Harvard, Lisa at Johns Hopkins. Or maybe it was the other way around.

Anyway, that was after. Fran and Don's kids were seniors in high school when all this started. Fran had just served them plates of fried fishsticks and hash browns when she detonated her nuclear bomb on the kitchen table. Don was still at work. "Kids, I'm divorcing your father and intend to live with Lena Gold—whom I love—as soon as she is released from prison, where she is being wrongly held. As soon as my writ of habeas corpus is approved by the Third District of the Appeals Court of the State of Illinois on the grounds of unconstitutional government entrapment . . ." There was a little *Get out of here with your law stories, Mom,* until they realized her earnest legal babble was dead serious. After this, there was a lot of shrieking and door slamming. What-the-hell's-gotten-into-you sort of stuff. But what was done was done. Their mother's voice didn't crack and she was matter-of-fact. "This is non-negotiable, but remember, I will always be your mother and your father will always be your father." Then Lisa and Jeremy took off in Fran's car, and she remained at the kitchen table with folded hands and waited for Don to return home. He took it better. Don endured the news, as he did every other setback in his life, with a baffled shrug. Fran, although shy, had always been unpredictable in small ways, particularly when it came to sex. He'd spent much of his adult life charting her desires, trying to keep up with her. In 1974 they bought a water bed. In the spring of '79 they attended a conference, called "Orgies for the Happily Married," in Scottsdale, Arizona. The year before, the Rosenkrantzes, Nina and Simon, had spent an interminable Memorial Day holiday in Fran and Don's bedroom. This, of course, was bigger and was going to ruin his life, but what could he say? *Our house? Our family?* Fran wasn't a cold woman, and in twenty years of marriage she'd never lied to him. She had always been steadfast in her love. Now her love had changed focus, dramatically. "I ache for her, Don. It hurts. I'll say that much. It hurts me not to be there with her this very second." Two days later, Don and Jeremy and Lisa moved into a rented apartment above Don's Century 21 office on Simonian. He accepted a generous cash settlement as well as a half life interest in the house, split between him and the kids. Fran also contracted to pay both Jeremy and Lisa's twenty-thousand-plus tuitions.

My mom told me most of this. Not about the murder plot itself. That part was in the *Chicago Sun-Times* for three days running. She told me the rest, though. She was in on all that. Nothing shocks my mother. When Fran Swanner told her that she'd fallen fast and hard for one of her clients, the infamous bouffant-haired husband-killer Lena Gold, and that she was divorcing Don and he was taking the kids—and that she was going to help raise Mrs. Gold and the hit man's child —I can see my mom waving away the complications and giving Fran one of her smothering hugs and sloppy lipstick smooches and gushing, "Oh, honey. I'm absolutely thrilled you're in love!"

I played a cameo role in the saga. I was Theodore's babysitter after he moved in with Fran. Theodore was a pretty normal kid, considering. A sweet kid who was always handing me presents like half-eaten strawberries. He was also quiet. He never cried while I watched TV. He was mostly content simply to play with his mother's old shoes. Best of all was that I got ten dollars an hour, which was six dollars more than the going rate in those years. And after she got paroled, Mrs. Gold always tipped me another five when Fran wasn't looking. Then she'd speak to me in a raspy whisper I have forever associated with the way women talk in prison. "Little Beth," she'd say, even though I was nearly as tall as she was, "go nuts with the extra." I always got the feeling that Mrs. Gold tipped me more for not being afraid and not passing judgment than for anything I ever did for Theodore. Whatever the reasons, having Lena Gold's money in my pocket made my neck sweat. I'd get pricked by the power of it passing into my hand from her long, spidery fingers. As though now I had license to do something dramatic, like break someone's car windows on the way home. Or better, let my gym teacher — Mr. Carl — see me naked in his shoebox office, with the door locked. Because I knew how much he ached for that.

And even after she got out of prison, Lena Gold still had all that big white hair. It looked the same as it did when I was ten and would see her squatting in her front garden. In hindsight, I know she was probably masterminding her plan to get rid of Big Jerry, right there among her impatiens and petunias. But if anyone deserved it, he did. Jerry Gold was a loud, crashing guy. A wildebeest in a Cadillac, as wide as his whale of a car, a Coupe DeVille with doors the size of Toyotas. He used to drive 85 down Paulina Street. I'd be riding my bike around no-handed on a Saturday and Jerry would come barreling my way, jamming his horn, a suburban Ahab roaring out his sunroof, "SIDEWALK! SIDEWALK!" I don't think there was anyone in our neighborhood, including the forever cloistered Mrs. Newton Rimwaller (whom my brother swears he actually saw once in the fall of '79), who was very sad to hear that Lena Gold had hired two guys to dress up as house painters and assassinate him while he sang and farted in the shower. I know a lot of us were sorry she'd failed so embarrassingly.

But as much as Lena Gold's story has fascinated me for

these years—the roller coaster element of it, the intrigue of such crimes and domestic upheavals amid the square-lawned primness of my suburban northwest Chicago—when I think back on it, I mostly think of Don, the real estate broker. He was the fawn in the headlights. He was the one the botched attempt really did end up killing. Inadvertently, true. And yes, not literally. My mom tells me he's doing just fine these days, still living above his office. *Oh, you know Don. He's a trooper's trooper.* But I think I know differently. Something broke in that man, something I doubt even all this time has been able to heal. I've had enough of my own blind sides to know that while it may be easy to clear away the wreckage, it's much harder to stop fingering your scars.

I last saw Don in the winter of '85, a year after Lena Gold's early release. I was sitting Theodore. Fran and Mrs. Gold were at the opera. It was a Friday night in February, around 10:30. Theodore was already asleep when the front doorbell rang, which was weird. Fran and Mrs. Gold's house on Cedar Valley Road was what my mom called a "forget knocking, barge in the back door" kind of house. A house where you didn't wipe your feet, and where you simply merged into the chaos: Mrs. Gold's cooking spatter, Fran's case files all over the place, Theodore's play shoes, Mrs. Gold's salsa music. Only the Jews for Jesus rang the front bell, and they were welcome, too. But that night it was late and silent, and I turned on the outside light and opened the front door to a pale, nervous, jacketless man. In the brightness I could see that he'd cut himself shaving. His chin was bleeding.

"Mr. Swanner?"

"Evening, Beth."

"Hi." I rubbed my sweater arms. It couldn't have been

more than ten degrees, and Don's shifting feet creaked in the ancient hard-packed snow.

"I'd like to take a walk around, if you don't mind. Just for old times."

I continued to stare at him. His quick small breaths were like puttering exhaust in the cold. I mentioned before that Don was courtly. A beautiful man, as far as men go, I overheard Fran once tell my mother. But this was post–John Wayne Gacy Chicago. I thought, What if this famously mild-mannered ex-husband turned spurned lover suddenly, finally, goes berserk and tries to strangle Theodore—the love child of his wife's ex-con live-in girlfriend—to death in his angelic sleep? Gacy the clown juggled at birthday parties. Gacy the politician shook hands with Roslyn Carter. The police found twenty-seven bodies in his crawl space. Lena Gold was a decorated Brownie troop leader at the time of her arrest. I was fifteen and one-third, and I was the babysitter. Don gazed at me with beaten, patient eyes as I stood in the front hall he used to sweep every Sunday.

"I'm not sure I can let you in," I said.

"Excuse me?"

"I'm not sure if it's okay."

Don examined the way I was squinting at him and figured out what my problem was. He saw that I had the potential to be afraid of him, and this made him laugh. "I know you're just doing your job, Beth. That you've got a responsibility." He held up his right palm. "I absolutely promise not to run off with the silver, and God strike me dead this moment if I would ever hurt a child." His eyes pucked out when he said that last part, and he wasn't laughing anymore.

I stepped aside. He thanked me and offered his hand. We

shook as if we'd made some kind of deal, but I wasn't sure what we were agreeing to. Though Don was at least six feet tall, his hand was so small and sweaty, so fightless, so unlike Lena Gold's, that I wondered if Fran hadn't cast him out because of his puny hands. I hovered behind him as he skulked around the house with his hands behind his back, as if he were taking a tour at the Art Institute or, more likely, some frighteningly realistic exhibition dedicated to his previous life. He paused at the bulbous umbrella holder in the back hall. He nudged the faded green Oriental rug back into position. He reset the grandfather clock to match the time on his own watch. After trailing him for ten minutes, I went back to the den. I turned the sound down so I could listen to him creep around the kitchen. I heard him open the refrigerator, as if a look at Lena's strange and healthy foods (tofu, eight varieties of beets) would somehow explain what had gone wrong. For another ten minutes I heard nothing. I imagined him in a chair at the kitchen table, silently weeping with his head in his hands, antagonized by memories of Fran, pantless and beckoning, clad only in one of his dress shirts. Then, from the living room, I heard the loud swipe of a kitchen-size match. I was certain that he'd at last gone over the edge and had poured gasoline all over the furniture and that Theodore and I were done for, as good as charred. When I skidded into the living room in my socks, Don was squatting before the fireplace, feeding kindling to budding flames. He twisted around and looked at me.

"Thought I'd warm the place up a bit. Okay with you?"

"I guess so."

He rubbed his hands together. "It's been so long since I made a fire. I used to make—" He stopped and clapped.

"Hey. I'll bet you could whoop my butt in a game of chess. How about it, Beth?" His face was redder than it had been at the door, and his voice was suddenly too perky, as though he was trying desperately to be chipper, to be light. He went to the cabinet above the stereo. "We used to keep the chess set right in here, and maybe—" He yanked a cardboard box, turned around, and shuffled the plastic game pieces at me.

"Sorry, I don't play."

He turned back to the cabinet. "Scrabble? Now, there's a game. I know we've got a Scrabble board somewhere in here." He started dropping game boxes on the floor. Chutes and Ladders. Connect-Four. Gnip-Gnop. Othello. Life. Battleship. Then he laughed. "Christ, Parcheesi! Whenever my brother Burt drove up from Louisville—wait, ah ha!" He held up the Scrabble game in triumph. His goofy pained face was like a child's, more like Theodore's when he pressed chewed fruit into my hands than an adult with a job. He unfolded the board on the coffee table.

"I've got to call a friend," I said.

Don set the box on the carpet and looked at the fire. "Of course," he said. "I understand."

"It's kind of an important call."

"Right." He sniffed and checked his watch. "Anyway, I'll just sit here awhile."

"Maybe I'll play later," I said, to give him hope. I walked backward and watched him pull letters out of the box, slowly, one at a time.

Then I went back to the den, picked up the phone, and pretended to call a guy from school. His name was Evan Magocini, and he'd never so much as wiped his snot in my direction in four years. He had blond bristly hair like the end of a brand-new broom. I despised him and lusted after him.

"Hello, Evan," I said, loud enough for Don to hear. "I want you to know I despise you and everything you stand for." I paused and waited for Evan to respond as the operator told me to hang up and please try again. "Another chance!" I shouted. "You want me to give you another chance? What is this, *Wheel of Fortune*? Am I supposed to sit around and wait for you to get done foaming at the mouth over Luana Palandri?" I paused as the phone began to whine a tone like our school tornado drill. "No, Evan," I screamed, forgetting about Theodore sleeping upstairs. "No! Never!" Then I rammed the phone into the cradle. The house was still. Don didn't come running. He had his own misery and he didn't want to join mine.

But God, did I want him to. Because even though he tried to laugh, he didn't pretend. Sorrow was in his hands, in his eyes, in the blood on his chin, and I wanted to touch it. I wanted to do more than touch it. It would have been my first time, and I thought how right that would be. Another legacy of Lena Gold. She'd probably have approved. A little love for two who needed it. And I knew he would be gentle. Those teeny fingers unbuttoning my jeans, the same slow way he was picking up those letters, poking my buttons through the penny slits, one after another. But what if he refused me? What if after I went to him and nuzzled close and pushed the Scrabble board out of the way with my knee, he only smiled graciously and said, "Well no, Beth. I couldn't." I sat on that blue velour couch and listened to the cackle and spit of the fire in the living room and could not move. I sat and waited in front of the silent television for Don to do something, anything, to acknowledge me again. To say, Beth. To say, Beth, help me. To say, Beth, I want you to help me. I watched the silent television.

When Mrs. Gold clattered into the room in heels, fur, and white leather, Don was gone and the fire had burned down to ashes.

"Honeybaby," she said as I stared droopily at her tower of hair. "You're getting beautiful. Since when all of a sudden are you getting beautiful?"

3.

FALL RIVER MARRIAGE

At Horseneck Beach

SHE'S WEARING a daisy-patterned yellow one-piece and an enormous blue hat and she's rubbing sunscreen on her husband's flubby back. He's got a cigarette drooping out of the side of his mouth, and he's so pale he looks like he spent the last thirty years in a basement. She slides her fingers under his waistband. He leaps and yelps, *For crying out loud, woman, on the beach in front of all these people!* She hands him the bottle. Now do me. He takes the bottle and squeezes a burble of lotion into his palm. Then he breaks an egg on her head, one hand cracks his lotioned fist, and he slithers both hands past her ears. She does not scream, just says quietly, I'll kill you you fat bastard. He shakes the remaining contents of the bottle on his own head and musses his hair. Now both have shampoo-lather heads. She takes his hand and says, I should have married Bea Halprin's brother, Aubrey, the dead one. *Let's swim,* he says. He'd have croaked by now and I'd be living on State Farm. *I said let's swim,* he says. They walk to the edge of the water and linger there. That wasn't funny about poor Aubrey, he murmurs, as his wife, who is Sarah, dives and shrieks into the cold June Atlantic blue.

Sarah

THE THRILL of murdering her mother's plants. It comes back to her while pushing her baby daughter's wicker carriage down Everett Street. Something about the wind and the shadows of the trees and the frightening radio reports makes her think of her father's doom. She was twelve, and her father was smothered under piles of blankets on his deathbed, except that he wouldn't die. And nothing could convince her that her mother hadn't put him there. So she'd stomped across the house and yanked up all the plants by their roots, and run outside, tearing at her own hair as if it too were a plant. Her mother wondered to the doctor, who was in the house attending her father, if her daughter wasn't possessed by something. "She's always been an hysterical girl. It's been known to happen in this town, you know." And the doctor sipped his tea and laughed, but held off saying anything out loud about Lizzie Borden in a house so full of death already. Instead, he said, "The girl's grieving, Frieda. Let her be." But the idea made Sarah smile, too, standing in the long brown grass beneath the open kitchen window, listening. The idea of wielding that famous ax was not all that unappealing. Hadn't Uncle Solly told her that when he was a boy he delivered newspapers to Lizzie herself's door at Maplecroft, and that she always gave him dimes and pats on the head, even if she did do it? And everybody knows she did it, Uncle Solly said. So you could still be good after doing something like that. If she did it, she promised herself, she'd spare her baby brother.

"He isn't dead yet, Azariah," her mother answered the doctor.

And she remembers not hearing what the doctor said back, because she was already running, running down the cobbled streets, barefoot, stubbing her toes, hating her mother, and at the same time knowing how right she was — that no, he wasn't dead yet, that he was going to linger in that bed with that goat, the maid, Lillian, sponging his head forever, and she'd never be free to blame *her* finally and absolutely for doing it to him, for all those years of haranguing that drove him upstairs to bed for good. Her father retreated, skulked away from living; he didn't flee.

Now she looks at her own daughter, her Rhoda, bonneted, curled up, huddled in blankets, one foot sticking out over the edge of the carriage. One little leather shoe. Walt made such a game about shining her shoes with spit and polish. A daughter of mine's gotta look her best gorgeous!

Again she sees herself sprinting across these bleak streets, into and out of muddy puddles. Her bleeding feet numb. There was a war on, just as there's one brewing now, and she remembers thinking then she'd just as soon all the soldiers die, if her father had to die. Because, though she knew nothing of what men do after they fight wars, she could see them coming home already, alive, those marching men she saw from atop her father's shoulders, to flowers and songs. She could hear her mother praise them. And her father will still be upstairs, not dead but dead, and she'll still be a girl who's lost everything.

She remembers running and being happy she killed those plants and sorry the doctor didn't agree with her mother, sorry he didn't say, Yes, Frieda, maybe this girl is possessed by demons. Because she wanted Dr. Buffington to examine her the way he did her father. Wanted him to poke her and look under her eyelids. She wanted to be the one, not her father, to rub her sores and rub her sores and rub her sores. It should be her in that bed wrangling, kicking off the covers (he was always either too hot or too cold), wheezing like an exhausted horse, rubbing. The one with *Lupuserythematosus*. A word she practiced saying, over and over. Such a huge and ugly word for a laughing, big-eared man. She wanted to be the one upstairs in the bed while her mother, in the kitchen, moans that the noise is killing her: My husband dying of a woman's disease.

Sarah wanted to be the one that stupid Lillian sponged and cooed.

A mother now, a wife now, but the streets will always be the same. Farragut. Gardner's Neck. Weetamoe. Massasoit. Wampanoag. Running, toes bleeding. She could never get far enough away. The baby shakes the bonnet off in her sleep. Her father died. The soldiers came home. Her mother still won't look at her baby.

Walt Kaplan Reads Hiroshima, *March 1947*

H E sits in a creased maroon leather recliner with his feet flat on the rug. The book is slender, nearly weightless in his hands. The door of his tiny study is closed. He reads by the light of a lamp that sits on a dark oak desk, now cluttered with a few opened books, face down. Otherwise the desk is tidy, with a lone paperweight in the shape of a terrier (the same one he once tried to glue to the hood of his Ford in a dig at Cy Friedman and his Cadillac DeVille), a heavy-duty stapler, a leather-bordered blotter, and a small framed photograph of his daughter as a baby. His wife, Sarah, gabs in the back yard with Erma Friedman—he can see them from the room's single window—the ladies stand, wavy dresses in the gust, by the huge boulder that looms oddly between the two houses. It is late afternoon, Saturday. He reads. By page 13 the flat nonchalant terrorless prose begins its scream. *Everything flashed whiter than any white.* He reads.

No one could say that Walt's not a patriot. In the war he was 4-F. Wife and daughter plus extreme asthma. So he joined the Civil Defense. His job was to make sure people retreated to their houses, to their basements, when the air-raid sirens shrilled. Walt Kaplan, rooted in the middle of Weetamoe Street with his steel helmet loose on his head, ordering and pointing. A starter's gun loaded with blanks jammed into the waistband of his pants, the idea being that if people didn't move fast enough he could fire into the air. Once he'd threatened to do it when that loony Roland Shutan refused to stop mowing his lawn. Walt had raised the little gun above his head but hadn't fired, and though the gun made him almost a soldier, he never liked the weight of it in his palm.

And though the 4-F made him a coward and he despised it with every ounce of his soul, he couldn't picture himself firing on anybody, even Rollie Shutan, even with a gun that shot only blanks. A man with a wife and daughter killing anybody. But didn't Melvin Zais have a wife and son, and didn't he die in Italy, a married hero with a son to worship his photograph? Didn't scrawny Mel Zais die with a gun in his hands? Mel Zais, who worked alongside him at J. J. Newbury's and later at his father's store, who lived at 618 ^{1}/$_2$ Tuttle Avenue his whole life, even after he married Irene and they had Toby, dying at Anzio with a gun in his hands, sweet Italian soil in his mouth and a single Fascist bullet in his temple. Now, in this thickened quiet of 1947, when he no longer is called to the street (he keeps the little gun in his drawer), he reads of Truman's bomb, more than twenty-thousand tons of TNT, atomic, and Father Wilhelm Kleinsorge in his underwear. He reaches the bottom of page 48.

To Father Kleinsorge, an Occidental, the silence in the grove by the river, where hundreds of gruesomely wounded suffered together, was one of the most dreadful and awesome phenomena of his whole experience. The hurt ones were quiet; no one wept, much less screamed in pain. No one complained; none of the many who died did so noisily; not even the children cried; very few people even

Walt stops near the top of 49, remembering the number, not folding in an ear. He balances the little book on the arm of his chair. Father Kleinsorge, no hero, a German Jesuit priest in Japan, a thin, lethargic, bent-over cornstalk of a man. The man was sickly even before what Hersey calls the noiseless flash. Walt leans his head back over the top of the chair and stares at the ceiling and knows it's lunacy, probably worse, sacrilege, an insult to the suffered, but he envies Father Kleinsorge. Envies him in his underwear in a country not his own amid the mute death, bodies under every bridge, on the banks of all seven rivers of Hiroshima. Frighteningly silent children coughing and dying in the smoke of Asanto Park. Sarah would say, Walter B. Kaplan, time to get your over-heated noggin examined by Dr. Gittleman, some parts are grinding down already. And Father Kleinsorge clawing through the splintered wood of a ruined house for a voice faintly calling, and Walt Kaplan in the middle of Weetamoe Street with a whistle and a pretend gun. A child's toy. A track-meet popper.

He stands and walks the tiny room, pausing at the Kaplan Brothers' Furniture Store calendar that hangs on a thin nail by the window. His father, Max, and his two uncles, Irv and Yap, in fancied-up oval pictures, his father frowning, his little uncles grinning: Have we got a deal on a sofa and loveseat combination for you, Mr. and Mrs. Oblinski, yes, we do . . . A two-year-old calendar, still on February 1945.

Walt Kaplan, thirty-one years old and already his back hurts, his hair barely clings; he feels as if he's peeking through a crack in the door on fifty. A soft-spoken man who after a couple of drinks will laugh and tell Old Fall River Line stories for as long as his friends and brothers-in-law will listen. Built a bar down in his own basement for that very reason. So he'd never have to worry about the bar closing on a story. That, and with a bar in his own basement, Sarah gets to keep one ear on him, and so long as he can drink a little and mostly talk, he doesn't care that he never gets to go to Orley's. *Walty K.'s Home Front,* Alf and his brother Leon still call it down there. Three chrome stools with red vinyl coverings. Heavily varnished bar top and Walt's famous mermaid swizzle sticks hidden in a coffee can behind the old cash register. A big man, roly-poly since he was a kid. For the most part he carries it well—though stairs have always been a huffer and he fights to keep his shirt stayed tucked. Loves and fears his wife, adores his daughter to death.

He doesn't ache for the bravery. The reaching into flames, so unfathomable—seared flesh sliding off grabbed hands and Father Kleinsorge, not repulsed, holding on to what was left and pulling. No, something far more simple. Walt's astonishment that Father Kleinsorge had vigor left to save. That his energy even half-matched his instincts. Walt stares at his dead father's now berating eyes. Then at his father's crumpled-faced brothers, the little bachelors who worked like dogs to please Max, who haunt the store even now, bitty wizened ghosts hovering among the lamps in the storeroom.

He thinks, I would have collapsed in a fat heap had they beat us to it and dropped it on Fall River. The Japs or the Germans.

The Civil Defense patrol captain for Ward 9 (Weetamoe Street to the 300th block of Robeson), me with my 4-F and cursed asthma and my Sarah and my Rhoda, and I would have wheezed and gasped. Would not have run from the chasing fire with babies in my arms. I am six years younger than Father Kleinsorge. I would not have saved my wife and daughter and the Minows, and the Friedmans, the Ranletts, the Bickles, the Pfotenhauers, the Eisensteins, the Corkys, and goddamn Rollie Shutans. A hundred thousand people writhing and shrieking, dying American style, the two onion domes of St. Anne's exploding, both the Quechechan and the Taunton blazing, and I would have been under the Ford, whistle in my mouth, gun in my useless hand—

Sarah knocks gently on the door. But as is her way—to remind him that her deference to his private study only goes so far—she says loudly, accusing, "What are you doing?"

"Reading, Sarah."

"Reading Sarah? What'd I write?"

He laughs. "Don't come in here."

"We're meeting the Gerards at the Red Coach at 7:30."

"The place that's shaped like a caboose?"

"Seven-thirty."

"Rhoda?"

"She's going to stay at Ida's. Gabby's over there. We'll swing by on our way home."

"Fine."

Sarah stays at the door for a couple of moments, stoops, and looks at him through the keyhole. His back is to the door, but he knows what she's doing because he heard her knees snap and her breathing sound closer. One time he taped over the hole with black masking tape, but she poked through it with a pencil.

"I said it's all fine, Sarah."

Her feet clump heavily down the stairs—his wife is no breezy chicken feather either. Without looking back at the little book, Walt opens his closet. He keeps his shoes and suits in his study. He picks up a shoe, takes it out of its felt sleeve, and inhales a big whiff of the polish. No smell like it in the world. All his shoes smell this good. Like taffy apples soaked in dye.

Sarah tromps back up the stairs. She didn't like something in his voice. As though their conversation through the door never ended, she says, "What are you reading?"

"Nothing, Sarah."

"Walt."

"About Hiroshima. The Hersey book."

"The one where we're supposed to feel sorry for the Japanese?"

He opens the door. "Sarah, you don't know."

His wife is crimson and anxious, standing in the narrow hall. She is thirty and raised a child during war (she used to send Walt out to trade vegetables for extra candy rations), got news of her sailor brother Albert's death at New Guinea in a letter from the War Department, her being his older sister, his closest living relative. Not to mention Pearl Harbor. Not to mention what the Nazis did to Jews. Who needs more sorry? We've got enough sorry as it is. This man. So swayed by newspapers and books as if they were God and everything those men wrote in them was always true. As if what they said were more true than her framed letter from the War Department: *With love of country and utmost valor.* Has to crack him on the head sometimes to pull him out from under that reading. And she used to watch him from behind the blackened curtains of the kitchen window, standing bowlegged in the middle of the street with that whistle and helmet playing General George Patton, warning neighbors in a tone of voice they never heard from Walt Kaplan before: *Citizens, if this was a genuine air raid, you'd have approximately six minutes and forty-five seconds.* Those days, when the papers shouted U-boat in the Cape Cod Canal and scared all the old fishermen out of their bananas. Everybody watching out for periscopes in their toilets.

Walt looks at Sarah, his face drained of color, bleached, like a drowned child. *Rhodas. How many thousand daughters reaching and that priest wasn't even in the Civil Defense.*

Sarah watches his stricken face, so close to hers, so familiar, so changing, withdrawing. His shoulders tremble. He's holding a shoe. Afraid of what, Walt? What? You beautiful cowering man, already old in the eyes. You'll die before I do and leave me in this house and the silence from the basement will kill me. Shhhhhhhhhhhhhhh! You drunken whozits are waking the baby!

"Walt," she says. "Hold still. Hunk of sleep in your eyes the size of China. Telling me I don't know. Hold still." Sarah fingers the yellow schmutz out of the edge of his eye with a nail. Then she pulls her finger down his cheek and lets go.

Melba Kuperschmid Returns

MELBA KUPERSCHMID was a beautiful one, and everybody knows what happens to the beautiful ones. Scooped up and gone before she turned twenty. He was a traveler; nobody even knew his name or what he did for a living, only that he had daring and never lived in one place for very long. But her old friend Sarah Kaplan used to get postcards from places that didn't seem very romantic from the photographs. Windsor, Canada, for one. St. Louis, Missouri, for another. Then, twenty-three years after she left, as everybody claimed they knew in their heart of hearts would happen sooner or later, Melba Kuperschmid came home. Discarded like the beautiful ones always are, one way or another. But when she came back to Fall River, she wasn't fat like everybody expected. She was still gorgeous. Still had all that hair and those enormous black eyes men fell into, flailing. Still Melba, not destroyed, even a little giggly, like she always was. Not lamenting being deserted, not even discussing it.

For a few months she went to cocktail parties and talked (politely) to the husbands, letting everybody know from the way she refused to laugh at the men's bad jokes that she wanted no part of them. This of course made a lot of the wives suspicious. What else could a returned (spurned, vanquished) divorcee possibly want if not their potbellied husbands? The other curious thing was that not long after she came home (she had no family left, and she'd had no children) Melba—now in her mid-forties—opened a seamstress shop on Corky Row, apparently with her alimony money. She'd always been good at sewing, a lot of the girls remembered that. But Melba Kuperschmid? A dressmaker?

Sarah had always loved her. As girls they often left school in late morning and spent afternoons trudging the mud along Watupa Pond. Slogging and cackling about people. They used to talk about what they'd do when they got to Paris. Twirl in the streets, first of all. Then search for dark, Mediterranean men with unpronounceable names and wispy, tuggable mustaches. For Sarah, Melba's return was a strange jolt. She'd been marching forward. She'd raised Rhoda into a girl people talked about (Rhoda had been elected "most garrulous" and "best dancer" by her class at Durfee). Sarah had served as volunteer chair of the hospital charity luncheon eleven years in a row, and was a respected member (and past treasurer) of the Hebrew Ladies Helping Hand Society. The new house on Delcar wasn't so new anymore, but the mortgage was far from dead and buried. There was Walt and his cars. He talked about his old junked cars as if they were children who'd grown up and gone away. Now he was in love with Volvos, which made him, according to him, avant-garde. Rhoda already in her fifth term at Simmons the year Melba came home, 1961.

Was it really possible that Melba wanted nothing more

than to open a shop and live quietly, modestly, in a rented apartment mid-hill? Sarah tried to distance herself from the gossip of the girls. There were all kinds of explanations. Dotty Packer said that some cousin of Leddy Levine (of the Harry Levines) told her that Melba's ex-husband was a gambler who fled because he was wanted by J. Edgar Hoover *and* the Sugar House Gang for extortion and unpaid debts. Somebody else—Ruth Gerard—said Melba's husband was a kind of junior-issue sheik who got summoned back to Arabia to marry a sultan's first-born daughter. That was a good one. Ruth Gerard always came up with good ones, and Sarah chose not to add that she had in her possession an old photograph (Melba had sent it from the Midwest somewhere) of the man she married and he was white as white could be, bare-chested, leaning against a tree, wearing a bowler and a crimped smile that made him look like he was being pinched, but oh, was he handsome, very. The only thing Sarah would offer the gossip eaters was a lie she claimed she'd heard from Tenelle Donnatello (who was considered close to the new Melba because it was from her husband, Felix, that Melba rented shop space) that Melba had left him, not the other way around. This of course prompted Bea Halprin to huff, "Well, in that case, where's her other man? And why come back here if life was so wonderful she could ditch him in the first place?"

The fact was that nobody knew because nobody asked. Even the most fearless Nosey Parker, Edi Dondis, didn't have the courage to broach the subject directly. Because there still floated about Melba a halo of untouchableness, an aura that went beyond her physical beauty into realms no one could describe in conversation. She'd had it since she was a child, and everybody recognized that it still shrouded her with as much force as ever. (For example, they all started wearing hats indoors again.) Yet since Melba was something of a shopkeeper now, it became a question of class. This didn't bother Sarah, of all people, but it did, after a while, make it more awkward to invite her to cocktail parties, and eventually most of the girls stopped asking her to most gatherings, except the occasional low-profile non-charity luncheon. And when this didn't appear to ruffle Melba's feathers, some of the girls started saying, Maybe there's something wrong upstairs. Didn't something like this happen to Sylvia Zagwill's brother Jerome, that one morning he just refused to get out of bed ever again? There was a lot of dispute on this point, because even those girls who stopped sending over invitations still took their dresses down to Melba to be fitted or let out. First, out of pity, they took things they no longer wore. Later they relied on her because she was so good they couldn't live without her. Finally the consensus was that anybody that excellent with the needle (particularly after all these years) couldn't possibly be crazy. But that didn't make the socializing problem any easier for anybody.

About eight months into Melba's return, Sarah parked the big Lincoln Town Car on the street in front of the house on Delcar. (Walt always insisted she drive his past loves; this one was so huge it didn't fit in the garage.) But she didn't get out of the car. Instead, she paused and reflected that she'd just spent a good chunk of her time at the market worrying over the mystery of Melba Kuperschmid: her lack of bitterness, her lack of interest in reclaiming any former glory. They had all been so jealous—she was the envy of a thousand girls—it must have been real. Now her coming home and not caring a lick threw everything into question. The way she used to walk the halls, as if stepping on puddles of air nobody else could see, the boys quivering and gnawing their collars. Sarah left the groceries in the car and went in the house to look for something that needed mending. Not finding anything, she went into Walt's closet forest of white shirts and ripped the sleeve of one. Got back in the car, melting strawberry ice cream and all (this was in August), and headed down the hill to Corky Row. She found Melba behind the counter, alone, her back to the door, working the Singer, the clicking monotonous, feverish, loud enough for her not to hear Sarah open the chimeless door.

And Sarah stands mesmerized by the back of Melba's head. Her hair is pulled back tight in a plait; its end rests on her shoulder. Sarah looks at the exquisite column that forms that familiar neck. If she could freeze a moment in time, she'd freeze this one, the one before Melba turns around and sees her, because it isn't the new Melba she wants, it's the old one, the one who left here looking for something better. To ask what it's like to be so loved that rolling your tongue around your teeth's enough to make men swoon and need cold water. *And that still not enough for you.* Melba, with your simple black hair and big eyes, still no breasts to boast to the Queen of Sheba about, and yet you're Melba, aren't you? Aren't you? You were two years ahead of me. And you used to whisper that you stole a pack of Mr. Jalbert's cigarettes. *Come on, Sare. We're as good as gone!* And that was all it ever took.

In the shop, pressing her handbag and the shirt to her chest, listening to the manic click of the machine, watching Melba's head. Maybe Sarah will tell her again (she wrote her about it after, in a flurry, and sent the letter to one of the many addresses she had for Melba then) about her own escape from Fall River. She's sure Melba's forgotten, if the letter even made it to her. And of course it was only for a weekend, but there was Sarah Gottlieb's famous eloping to Rhode Island. People still talk about how Rhoda was born big and healthy barely six scandalous months later, and how her mother's rage lasted till the day she died. Didn't Sarah take her risk, too? She never thought it would matter again (today she was just like so many other people), but now her once running means more.

She clears her throat. "Melba dear, I thought I'd drop by and bring you—"

Melba swivels her stool. Slivery wrinkles below her eyes like veins in a leaf the only change. It could be 1936. They could be on the shore of Watupa Pond talking about Howie or Hughie, the one from Boston who chased Melba for months, one of the many she didn't choose, the one who kept circling her block in his convertible, hundreds of times. They called them Howie's laps, and they became as much a part of the neighborhood as Mrs. Gilda Rubover's garden of rabbit skeletons.

Yes, the same as ever, but tired now, too. Maybe it's the sallow light of the store, but there's exhaustion in that still-beautiful face. Melba's eyes linger before she welcomes Sarah with her old closed-mouthed smirk. It's in the way the sweat's pooled in the notch of her upper lip. A glimpse of what's disappeared in that trickle of moment before Melba calls, sprightly, over the noise of the machine, "Ah, Sarah. You brought me some mending."

And Sarah looks at her and thinks, We're becoming older

women, on the verge of turning into those fat-ankled wad-
dlers at the club, the ones that Walt says keep disappearing
into their shoes. Even you.

Melba waves her closer. "Sit! Sit!" The shop is cluttered
and stuffy. Fabric's stacked in piles on the floor. Skirts are
clipped on hangers draped over ironing boards. Measuring
tape's in a heap. There are books on a shelf alongside a pile of
sewing magazines. There's a bowl of chocolate and a ripped
calendar. A cat. *Even you, Melba. You can't hide behind not
caring.*

Melba tosses a pincushion away, wipes off a wooden
school chair with a rag. "Sit! Sit! For God's sake, sit down,
Sarah." She sighs. "So good to see you. Too too long. I haven't
laid eyes on you in weeks, ages, honey."

Sarah sits on the edge of the chair to make clear she can't
stay long, that she's only pausing for a quick chat. She tells
her about the shirt, about what a klutz Walt is, how he insists
on wearing his good clothes around the house to fix things
that don't need fixing. Yet even as she rambles on, she becomes aware of something in the way Melba said "weeks,
ages." As if they aren't different. As if they could just as easily
be the same, for all she needs or cares. And then she knows,
all at once, what should have been the obvious truth all
along: that the marriage was short-lived, that the husband
probably didn't last a year or two after that shirtless picture by
the tree, that it was Melba who did all the moving around,
that she'd been alone, that she'd been a dressmaker for the last
twenty-odd years, a damn good one, and that she came home
for the same reason everybody comes home, but that in her
case it wasn't to chase her past; she merely wanted to live near
it. That proximity itself was comfort.

That she'd been alone, probably many years alone, maybe even because she wanted to be. Sarah thinks of Walt, how often during the day she forgets about him, but how he arrives every afternoon, breathing heavy at the back stoop, arms full of more junk they'd never need; but he arrives, always, some afternoons knocking on the door with his head because he's got no free hand. And yes, she feels pity, but Sarah's first instinct is to rub Melba's unchanged face in everything she doesn't have, to unbuckle her handbag and wave pictures of Rhoda. Rhoda's report cards, her hundred boyfriends, her Honor Society pins, her still-life drawings of fruit and vegetables . . .

They make small talk about the shop and some things Melba's working on. She's doing Nina Shetzer's daughter's wedding party. *(An absolutely horrid plum! The bridesmaids are going to look like the walking wounded.)* But after a couple of awkward, too-long silences, Sarah can't keep herself from blurting, "I hate myself for saying this, Melba, but the girls all talk about your life like it's a train wreck."

Melba laughs and swoops her arm in an arc to dismiss them all, every last one of them, to hell. And what's incredible is that even her voice is the same, thick and direct like a man's, like the rocks she used to fling into the Watupa. "Tell them I was never a whore. Tell those yappies that."

Sarah doesn't nod, only stares back at her and seeks forgiveness from Melba's eyes for the curse of being no better than everybody else, for reveling in such a miraculous and perfect failure. She thinks of the early postcards, the black-and-white photographs, Melba's zigzagged scrawl: *Darling Sarah, We've moved to a place called Wabash in Indiana. We live in a house on a small hill overlooking a dirty rushing river. Re-*

minds me a bit of home, but the rivers are so much smaller here. Please write! I don't know two souls here. Your M

"Not one of them ever once called you that. Not one."

But Melba's still laughing at the thought and doesn't care if they did or they didn't. She scoots her stool closer, leans, and squeezes Sarah's wrists. Her palms are hot and wet from work.

Birth of a Son-in-Law

A ND THEIR DAUGHTER married Arthur Mendlebaum.
The wedding was at Beth El in Fall River, and Walt and
Sarah Kaplan were dressed to the nines, beaming. Sarah di-
recting traffic, Walt telling jokes he either read in a book or
stole from Alf Dolinsky. Rhoda one enormous smile in white
—though to Sarah's horror she'd pinned up her train at the
last moment. Arthur's family, cranky rich Rhode Islanders
who looked down their noses at Fall River, at the musty temple, at the murmuring rabbi in his soup-stained jacket. At the
Kaplan relatives and their Russian accents, at Walt's made-up
Yiddish that was really pigeon Portuguese he'd picked up
from stock boys at his store. But Arthur himself was a peach,
a good old boy who could pal around with Walt until Walt
exhausted himself with stories. Sarah said Walt loved Arthur
more than Rhoda, if only because Arthur was the first person
in Fall River history who'd never once yawned in his face, said
she'd be happy if they'd have him down to New York to take
the load off her ears once in a while. Of course, this was bull;
at home, with nobody around, it was Sarah's yap that drilled
holes in his ears and Walt who'd hunker in his study with his
maps and atlases. But talk is talk at a wedding, and Walt said,

"Anytime I'm invited I'll come down there and bore Arthur to so many tears he'll sleep in his office to escape me." And Arthur said, "For God's sake, Walt, you're the least dullest guy from here to Worcester" (pronouncing it Worster), and everybody yucked as if he was the next greatest Jewish comic. Sarah laughed loudest, her patented guffaw, her whale honk. Arthur was taller than any Jew she'd ever known, much less been related to. He laughed because he liked to laugh. He pinched Rhoda when he thought nobody was looking. He looked at other girls when he thought nobody was looking. He was a healthy strapper who was going to be rich! Didn't everybody know he had a job working on the Stock Exchange in New York? Rich, rich, rich, rich, rich. Arthur is going to be rich and Rhoda is going to have babies and speak French to them. Why Rhoda went around speaking that French, Sarah had not an iota of an idea (though it was true that she often told her friends, "Well, you know, Rhoda is truly a genius at the French language"). All she really knew was that her daughter was going to have a house in the suburbs of New York, a real house with more than two trees and more than one bathroom. In a place called Rye Bread, Walt insisted on calling it. My daughter is leaving a city named after the mighty confluence of two rivers for a place named after a sandwich. But Rhoda said no, it was only called Rye. Rye, New York. A place with shaggy trees, wide boulevards, no dead mills (our rat hotels, Walt calls them) — a place with no jobs, only houses and trains. Trains to take men in hats to work in the city and trains to take them home.

The reception is in the basement of Walt's Elk Lodge. The two of them stand in front of the empty trophy case, watching. Walt elbows her. "Want another hot dog on a stick?"

"Yes."

"Another glass of champagne?"

"Yes."

"Kiss on the kissa?"

And Walt, hot dog–mouthed, kisses her and the people dance and her daughter floats by whispering elegant nonsense, and even the Elk's cheap chandelier is high-class. They've killed Kennedy and we might be in a new war. Nobody seems to know for sure except Walt, who says, "Absolutely we are, don't let anybody fool you, it's a war." Either way, all that counts is that Arthur's got two bum knees and glasses thick as dictionaries. Walt says they can't make him go anywhere. Rhoda's got the best figure of any girl here, even better than Dotty Packer's niece, the one marrying that hoodlum from Swansea. Arthur dances like Frankenstein's cousin. Walt chomps another hot dog on a stick, holds up the stick, and looks at it. "I could have invented this. I'd have bought you an island with the money."

Rhoda prances over like an excited colt. Her face is plump and cherry and maroon and pink from lipstick kisses. "Mother, I want you to dance with Arthur. I'll whirl Daddy."

Sarah closes her eyes and lets this giant sway her. His big hands grip her waist, and Lord, she feels things she shouldn't. She whispers, "Hurt a hair on her head and I'll pry out your eyes with a fork." Arthur cackles and squeezes her tighter, and she loves it, the squeezing. *The husband of my daughter only an hour.* She'll take this to the grave, but right now, Sarah lets it ooze through her like the champagne. She's exhausted and lusty, and what else is there in this world? Someone digs a long nail into her shoulder and whispers, "Congratulations,

Mrs. Mother-in-Law," and without opening her eyes she sees everything. Those snoots, the in-laws, hiding at their table, wishing they were back in Rhode Island; Walt hamming, doing his strange version of the rumba, while the rest of the room slow-dances to "Love Me Tender." So many cars in the Elk's parking lot people had to park over at the Al Macs. The bandleader's shoulders, tight in a tuxedo three sizes too small for him. The wiggle of the chandelier tears. The way they swing light. She created this. She never wanted an island. She wanted this.

Arthur's steamy chocolate breath on her neck, his limp and his bad eyes that protect him from people who want to send him away to get killed. And he will take Rhoda up in these arms tonight, but he won't smother her, even though he's so huge his Abraham Lincoln feet don't fit on the bed. She can hear his big shoes thump and the *tink tink* of Rhoda's white heels landing. And she can hear Rhoda sigh. Like her father, she's always been a melancholy girl. All of this will finally make her sad, and Arthur will know this but not understand. And Rhoda won't explain it to him because she doesn't know enough to explain. He will accidentally knock the clock over with a klutzy elbow, and Rhoda will grab him as he leans over and order, Leave it, the clock, leave it. And they will leave the clock on the floor and the light on, too, and they will love and push and grip and pull and wander and twist and love it and love it, and maybe hurt, too, in each other's bodies until finally exhaustion creeps and overtakes. But their sleep will not be peaceful, because in it they will leave each other. And before dawn they will wake up tired in the flood of lamplight, and for too many moments they will be wretched and wonder why silently, without telling the other, because they won't understand, because they're too young to understand, because it takes years to understand—she thinks of Walt, who will hide in the men's toilet and wheeze after this dance—why the morning will always be harder than the nights.

At the Conrad Hilton

WALT. Mesmerized by Uncle Alf Dolinsky's feet. Dolinsky is lying on his bed in his newly polished brogans, enjoying himself. What's there not to enjoy? It's summer and they're at the Conrad Hilton. Walt and Alf Dolinsky in Chicago for the National Furniture Retailer Association's annual convention. Yet there's a glitch. Walt's standing again for vice president. Nobody ever runs against anybody, the votes are a formality, only this year he's facing a challenge from an upstart barely out of his twenties, sells period furniture in Cincinnati. Alf says the kid's a maggot, sells antiques, for Christ sake, and hasn't got a Good Humor's chance in hell of getting elected. But Walt knows better. He's been around long enough to know that the only thing left to become after making it anywhere in this world is a has-been, and he's already served on the association's board ten years—was even president from '57 to '59—and now there's this pimple-face telling every buttonhole in the hotel lobby about the need for new blood. And the old blood? It's another death knell, the bell that's been donging in Walt Kaplan's ears for more years than he wants to remember. *Walt Kaplan? What ever happened to him? Guy could sell you the hole in a doughnut.*

"Period furniture," Walt says finally. "New stuff, just looks old. If he sold antiques, he wouldn't be a retailer."

"Only you could find a way to worry in Chicago," Alf says.

Walt doesn't move, only stands there bending back his thin, pale fingers—his father once said he had a woman's hands because they were so small and always cold. He's still entranced by Alf's clodhoppers. Dolinsky's greatest joy, lying on a bed in his shoes. Maybe this is why he comes on these trips in the first place, because if he pulled this at home, his wife, Doris, would bust his jaw. Uncle Alf, a real uncle once, to his nephew Gary, Charlie's son, the one who died exercising. Walt always knew that stuff would kill you.

"It isn't that."

"Isn't what?"

"The kid from Ohio."

Now it's Alf who turns silent, who stares at the ceiling, then the window. The city's below them, crawling lights and honks. Even up here they can hear the doorman whistling for cabs. The window's open, and a breath of damp wind grazes Alf's cheek. He watches it toss the drapes, billow them, and he thinks of a dress that once did that, furled as it turned away from him. A dress he once called Eva Pearlmutter.

"We've been friends how long?" Alf says.

Walt murmurs, "Long time."

"Gimme a figure."

"I don't know. Since McKinley."

"Thirty-four years and a month and a half. It was June your brother beat up my brother."

"All right, thirty years."

"So knock it off."

Walt paces. The room's got red carpet and white walls. They say every room at the Conrad Hilton's different, but his room is always the same: red carpet, white walls, brass bed. Not decorated like the kind of place for two wash-ups to be alone together, but being with Alf is almost the same as being by yourself, only slightly smarter. Besides, there's lots of times he'd rather be alone with Alf Dolinsky than Sarah, hotel room or no hotel room. Doris calls him the Flabby. She says, *Where's the Flabby today? Oh, the Flabby wants another piece of salami, doesn't the Flabby?* He works for Dave Rubin's cookie company, but his toughest job is being Walt Kaplan's best friend. They've already bought graves, side by side, in the newer old Jewish cemetery across from the Arco Station up President Avenue.

Alf cradles the back of his head and watches Walt clomp across the room, from the window to the door and back again. Alf talks to the ceiling: "Long time since we had one of these. A what's-it-all-for night! All right, Walt. You want the inventory or the philosophy first? I think we started with philosophy last time, so why not the inventory tonight?"

"Knock it—"

"Number one, your beautiful daughter Rhoda, cream of everybody's crop. Number two, your beloved wife, roaring Attila that she is; number three, your store, the grandest furniture palace this side of the Narraganset."

"I don't give a damn about the kid from Ohio."

"Then don't stand. Step down, retire, give a speech, let them give you a cheap watch."

Walt notices the lampshade on the night table's been burned by the bulb. Some maid turned it around so nobody would see it, but this place is crawling with furniture guys.

First thing we're going to do is inspect the accouterments. Classy operation. This place is world-famous? Still, he likes the way the frayed edge scallops the light on the wall.

Still pacing he says, "Like something in my brain's a little off. I got these ghosts in the corners of my glasses."

"Huh?"

"They follow me around. They're not anything I can see, they're empty. And they're not in the room, they're in my glasses."

"I don't get it."

"What's not to get? I see things and I don't see things."

"You're melancholy, Walt. Lots of guys are melancholy. Why don't you clean your glasses?"

"So much I feel like I miss, Alf."

"Like what?"

Without stopping, Walt shrugs. He reaches the window and spins. His face lightens. "Hong Kong."

"What about it?"

"I want to go there."

"So go."

"You don't want to go to Hong Kong?"

"I never thought about it."

"See, there's your problem. You lack imagination."

Alf adjusts his pillow, sighs. "It isn't Sarah? These ghosts in your glasses?"

Walt stops pacing. "Who said anything about Sarah?" He stands in front of the bed and looks down again at Alf, now into his face and also at his big ears, ears that have stuck out like a monkey's since he's known him. "Maybe I've got a girl," Walt says, "Porta-geese girl. Maybe I've got one in New Bedford."

Alf sits up, keeps his feet straight so that to Walt he looks like a fat mummy in expensive shoes. They'd planned to have a drink in the bar downstairs, go someplace for dinner, maybe take a walk down State Street and see the Marshall Field's windows. They've always gotten a huge kick out of Chicago, where selling's more of an art than it is in Massachusetts. Forget art, it's religion here, kill or be killed, and the old rules don't apply, and your name and pedigree don't matter a hoot to anybody. Christ, they let the Jews own half this city, including Sears Roebuck, although they keep Julius Rosenwald's name out of the name. Every other year the convention's in Chicago, and Alf, though he sells cream-filled cookies, not dinette sets, always joins him. Last time they gave Alf an honorary NFRA lapel pin. They've been friends how long? How many trips like this have they taken? But Walt's moody, always has been. Not that many people know it.

"If it's bothering you this much, take it to Jordy Tomason. He'll rig it. Jordy's not going to want that piglet yammering anyway. Never seen you so worked up about something like this. What do they give you, anyway? Some free magazines? Some wholesale discounts you'd probably finagle even if you weren't on the board?"

"How do you know I don't have a Porta-geese girl in New Bedford?"

In the room, it's getting hotter. Both men's hats are on the radiator. They look like big mushrooms. Alf watches Walt with the old sympathy, but also with bitterness. This happens sometimes — he sees his friend with his wife's eyes. Doris, who's never been satisfied. With the money Alf's father never had to leave them, with Alf never amounting to anything more than one of five vice presidents, with his not-so-secret lust over women long dead or who are so far away they may as well be. And now here's Alf with Dorry's eyes spoiling things at the Conrad Hilton, making him wish he'd had a better, stronger friend all these years, a man with more gusto, a man with more take charge, a man with—

"If it was a girl," Alf says, "it would be easy. If it was a girl, I'd cure you for nothing."

Walt breathes and steps back, lets the wall catch him. He slumps. Rambles on more to the carpet than Alf: "Not even twenty-one. Still lives with her mother and swears like a sailor. Got a little black mustache soft as the whiskers of Rhoda's dead cat. And legs, Alf, you should see her legs. Legs enough to make dead harpooners try to scratch out of their graves. Because she loves, Alf, swear to God, to dance in the old marine cemetery out near Pancher's Nursery. Her name is Edna, but she doesn't look like an Edna. Her parents wanted her to be an Edna, but she's no Edna. She's got spiff. She blazes. She's like the sun, Alf. The sun! 'A fair hot wench in flame-colour'd taffeta!'"

Alf looks at the floor, where there's one black sock. It could be either his or Walt's—there's no way to tell—they both shop for their socks at Pffaf's. To hell with Horseneck Beach, you can drown on Michigan Avenue, in nonsense, in Ednas who never breathed. Guy as big a walrus as I am, sinking into the fancy carpet. Alf would give him a hand if he could reach him from the bed.

Instead, he only pleads, begs, "Damnit, Walt. Chicago. We're in Chicago."

Awnings, Bedspreads, Combed Yarns

E YES SAUCERED by blue-gray half circles, Walt Kaplan watches them knock down City Hall in the name of progress. September 1971. The day is cloudless, the sky white. A helicopter dive-bombs like a horsefly and snatches the great gold eagle from the top of the dome and the crowd hollers, whoops, and the ball attached to the crane swings, the ball swings, and like a man defenseless against a sidelong punch from nowhere, the old granite eyesore begins its inward crumble. The roar after each hit like the loudest bowling he's ever heard. The men beside him on the sidewalk, in front of the post office, slap their hands and cheer and stomp their shoes and whoop some more. Nobody's seen anything like this. The ball swings toward them, a freakish pendulum, and everybody takes a couple of steps back.

Murder is what it is. In fifty years of being alive and walking these streets, how many times a day did he look at this building? Though Walt's known the worst times, he's always been one to climb the rungs of the pit. During the hurricane of '38, though he was young then, he'd laughed as trees took flight and roofs and chimneys landed in neighbors' yards. Even now, they still call him a crack-up, the genuine article, a real Wisenheimer. At the annual masked poverty ball at the Legion, who knew what he'd show up in. A couple of years ago he went as Salvini the Elder and Salvini the Younger at the same time, painted two extra eyes on his cheeks—all the women were screaming. Last year he somehow jammed himself into his sister-in-law's tutu. A man with half a million useless stories, Sarah says. (His favorite being how his father, dirty-faced Jewish kid from Lithuania, gets off at the wrong station, fifteen years old, and thinks he's in Boston, wanders around Fall River looking for Blue Hill Avenue in Dorchester. *And what doyouknow?* By the mid-twenties, Kaplan's Furniture's got the biggest showroom in the city by five thousand square feet. Branch stores at 344 Columbia and the corner of Pleasant and 4th.)

Beloved store that was his, Walt's, until ten days ago, when they knocked it down, too. Then there were no photographers, no police, no cheers, no helicopter swooping, only Walt, sweat-furious hands in his pockets, watching. "Exercising the state's right of eminent domain," the Department of Public Works lawyer had said slowly, arrogantly, as if the words were too difficult for a shopkeeper to understand. But he'd fought them for two years before he lost, in court, the right to own his own property. Then—because the law so ordered—they gave him a quarter of what the store was worth in the name of the good of the Commonwealth. *In this country!* You'd think Khrushchev was governor. And the idiot mayor proclaims Fall River will be a champion again. A return to the greatness of Spindle City, the Textile Capital of the World. That the new I-95 extension will be the greatest boon since Colonel Durfee opened his first cotton mill at Globe Corners in 1811.

The ball strikes, and the twin sets of pillars that lorded the front door crack and topple.

Of course he's not the only sap who knows that nothing they do is going to reopen a single mill. That a highway's so people can drive through Fall River, not to it. He doesn't corner the market on detecting bull when it froths out politicians' mouths. But others who know the truth, his brother, Leon, for example, gave it up. Leon, who is where right now? On a beach? *The government's going to build what the government wants to build. You forgotten the pharaohs? May as well dig up F.D.R. and blame him. May as well go fishing in the Taunton with your pinkie.*

But today, if nothing else, Walt insists on being up close to the destruction. This wafting of a hundred-some-odd years of undisturbed dust. He breathes it in like sniffing the rot at the back of Sarah's refrigerator.

And it goes far beyond the killing of his livelihood. That the route the DPW and the city council finally agreed upon went smack through Kaplan's, but somehow, like some miracle of Jesus, avoided Nate Lyons's Furniture Warehouse not a quarter mile away on Granite Block. Not to mention all the banks in town, and Sharder and Nolte's, Small Brothers, L. D. Wilbur's, Boyko Typewriters and Adding Machines . . . *Mr. Kaplan, be reasonable. All citizens, at one time or another, must make sacrifices for the sake of the common achievement . . .* That they forced him, a self-employed man, to go to work for Sarah's Fascist cousin Morris. That they turned him into a lackey with hardly an office, a peephole with a desk crammed in—with that little Führer speeching at him all day about how he's never met a man so lazy as Walt. ("That's how you lost the branches, kiddo. You're slow on your feet. Don't forget the highway didn't take away your daddy's branches. You lost them long before.")

The ball smashes the clock below the dome, the clock that was always slow. Everybody in town adjusted their watches to it, and Fall River was known as the town that was seven minutes off. How fast it takes to kill. There's an explosion followed by a loud sucking noise as the dome, screeching glass and grinding, caves in.

The joke is that nobody loves this city more. When he was a kid they'd say their pledge of allegiance, and then Mrs. Gerstadt would ask in singsong, Now, children, what makes our city so wondrous special? He can still chant the chant: Awnings, bedspreads, combed yarns, curtains, knitwear, shirts, sweaters, bathrobes, handbags, corsets, drapes, mattresses, braids, roll covers, sport clothes, thread, raincoats, plastics, furniture, luggage, underwear, industrial textiles!

Nearly blinded by the dust, sneezing, he finally turns away, and the clack of his shoes is empty defiance. But he'll take it. He laughs, and it scalds his throat. A funeral now, and I'm a mourner. Our fair City Hall. Born in 1845. The mother, a Flemish architect. Mrs. Gerstadt's toothless grinning: Not from Flemland, but from where? Children? Where does a Flemish person call home?

And didn't his father walk him through the long corridors, fingering portraits of dead old turkey-throated mayors as though the Buffingtons and Fozzards were Washingtons and Jeffersons? The echo beneath the dome. The way a whisper became a murmur became a shout.

He's due at work, but after what he's seen? Over the phone yesterday Leon said, "Why torture yourself? Get out of town for the day. Take Sarah to Boston. Buy her a steak at Jimmy's. Enjoy yourself half a day in your life. It's over, over."

Before his brother left, as the two of them were clearing out the last of the inventory and adjusting the books, Walt had snarled, "What kind of person moves to Florida to live?"

"Is that a question?"

"Enlighten me, grace me."

And Leon had sat in their father's ancient swivel chair and raised his legs and whirled the way they used to when they were stock boys. *Cause it's warm. Cause Bets loves it there. Cause her sisters live there, even though she hates them. Cause we've got the apartment in Fort Myers paid for. Cause they're driving the goddamned autobahn through our store. Because this town's not through dying. Cause I put a little money away. Unlike you. Cause it's warm.*

Not going back to the peephole today, because having to listen to that Morris would only drive the stake deeper. Cousin Morris, so kind to give you a job, Sarah says. You know he can't afford to go around giving handouts. How can you complain when it's honest work? And Walt saying, You don't understand, it's just talking. Moving money around. Not the kind of work I'm used to. Honest work, she says, as if his thirty-seven years of selling furniture was stealing from people.

Still listening to the crushing, preposterous war-like barrage, he walks down Third Avenue (avoiding South Main, where there's a hole where his store used to be) and across Rock Street. Then up Union Avenue. Halfway up the hill, the clamor becomes mercifully more faint, as though the tired clapboards are soaking up the sound. Christ Almighty, I'll stomp to Kansas City. Pains everywhere, but legs like tree stumps. He leans into the hill and marches. He salutes an old salty out on her porch, and she fumbles with her glasses and smiles. The decrepits always went for him. He could sell a newfangled recliner with all the bells and whistles to a crocker on her last legs. *Die with your feet up, my royal lady, and don't forget we now also carry Congoleum Rugs and Gruno Refrigerators.* He marches on. *Prices so low, your conscience will bother you.* He knows every tree stump, every graffiti initial. Knows who laid the cement for the sidewalk without looking down and reading the patinaed bronze plaque: O'CONNOR AND ANGELL, CONTRACTORS, FALL RIVER, 1893.

And he reaches 100 Delcar, and he's home but not home. Sarah can't see him, or there'd be all kinds of shrieking. What kind of man's not at work at 2:30 in the afternoon on a Monday? He creeps around back and hides behind the boulder. Collapses on the grass. He can hardly keep up with his own breathing as the damp seeps through his pants. The kitchen window's open. The Pooh-Bah's on the telephone. He feels the rock against his head. He sees the ball's slow hover and Sarah's plump fingers twisting the phone cord. Sees his brother spinning around in a chair in a room that no longer exists—and still Sarah talks. Our whole caboodle's getting bashed to hell, and it's caving, yes caving. But my scrumptious porkette's big mouth keeps talking. "I didn't tell her casserole was a bad idea, only that it might be wrong for the occasion, and she says why am I meddling in the food, and I said I'm overall chairman, and she says then why don't you worry about being chairman, and I said that's what I'm doing, worrying, and she says well, don't worry, and I said well, which is it, worry or don't worry?" He sinks further into the wet ground, loving her. He wants to climb in through the window and prance her around the kitchen bellowing like a lunatic, drag her upstairs, pull the shades, bite off her buttons, let the phone ring till it kills itself. And laugh, laugh. But he's a stowaway in his own yard, and also, much as he tries, much as he needs the rescue of it, he can't turn his quickened breathing into anything other than an old man's gasps.

High Priest at the Gates

WALT USED TO STAND outside the cemetery gates and smoke, because under some ancient law from the Talmud that he happily took advantage of, but never fully understood, he wasn't permitted to enter cemeteries, because he, Walt Kaplan, was a Kohen, a genuine descendant of high Hebrew priests. Of course he got a bang out of being royalty. He used to go around sometimes licking his finger and anointing people duke of this, duchy of that, even called Alf Dolinsky "my liege." When Dolinsky said that's not Hebrew, Walt said even the pope doesn't preach to his flock in Latin anymore. "Benevolent eminences like myself have to change with the times." Once, during Sarah's Aunt Ida's graveside service—Ida was so old for so long that most people forgot she hadn't died yet and were genuinely shocked when it happened—Walt put on one of those Burger King crowns and greeted people after the service with a gloved hand and a blessing, till Sarah whispered that if he didn't take that thing off in two seconds she'd rip his head off. But it was also out there with his pack of Kools, in front of the gates, across the street from the gas station, that Walt would ruminate on all the time he was going to have to spend inside the gates, among those graves, inside a cheap casket from Gould's. His status as a member of the Kohanim applied only to his living flesh; dead he was the same irrelevant schmo as everybody else. And even on the day Ida was disappearing into that irregularly mowed grass forever (he could hear Rabbi Gruber intone his stock line: "We shall always remember the cheerful countenance of the deceased"), he couldn't help comparing the time we spend here and the time we spend there, and working the whole thing out in his head for the nine millionth time and thinking again: Nasty joke. Here's your body. Now watch it die. Watching the crowd of mourners through the gates and wanting to shout that they all had it backward. Clowns, it's us, the ones still paying taxes, who need some honoring. It's the lucky stiffs in the ground—Ab Sisson, Teddy Marcowitz, Pearl Brodsky, Lou Jacobs, Hyman Sobiloff, and now even poor Ida—who should show more respect. They're the ones who should be huddled and bundled and murmuring and remembering. They're the ones who should be blowing snot in their hands. All Ida and the rest of the sleepers deserve is a handshake goodbye, maybe a peck on the cheek farewell, because for them it's a simple matter of going away, of leaving, of forgetting keys, wallet, driver's license, cash—an easy vamoose. You want sorrow? Out here! He wants to roar it at the backs of the mourners. Turn around! Out here beyond the gates, suckers! Turn around!

In the Dark

I N THE DARK she lights a match. She looks at herself in
the reflection in the window. The flame is jumpy and fickle
because she's breathing on it. Yet it stays lit until it burns
down to her fingers, and she watches herself in the uncertain
light and sees a face too large and blanched, like an unwelcome moon. The house so still and mute even the kitchen
clock's terrible grinding is muffled. She's downstairs in the
new room, the TV room, the room they remodeled in the
fifties. Walt's upstairs muttering out snores like a sea cow. It's
two o'clock in the morning and she whispers something even
she can barely hear: "What for?" What her mother used to
say, first thing she ever said in the mornings, even before her
father got sick, as though asking it of God. "What for? You
tell me what for?" Her mother who died of grief for a daughter who only ran away down the block. But why now? Why
Sarah asking? She thinks of Rhoda's tiny munching lips at her
nipples, remembers those grabby little hands—in this very
room—all that need. And now? It isn't that. She doesn't want
that need back. It's some other more undefined ache. Something else, like being haunted by the dying light of the
match. Haunted by herself, by her love, by her desire even

now to knead Walt's skin, even now to whisper in his sleeping ear—what?—that she's here, that Sarah's here, whisper, I'm here, I'm here. Because so much is occurring to her tonight and she can't sleep while the house drowses. Sarah lets the silence soak her into its blur, as if she were descending slowly through water. But she's never in her life been capable of whispering, of capturing a windless moment, and she fears he doesn't know this about her, that she can simply sit, in the dark, the radio off, and can, yes, can, consider that her life with him has been exactly that, a life, and life's not something you measure in good or bad. Her life with Walt a life—and if she could simply say—but that's not it either. He wouldn't want to hear about it, would shrug her away. "Whatayou talkin? Sarah? Whatayou talkin?" No, she would like to do it with a look that doesn't need explanation or interpretation, but instead would simply make him remember. He's such a writer down of things, such a holder on of nonsense; the man has files of pictures of furniture, of tables and chairs he sold twenty years ago—but there are so many things he doesn't remember, because he never thought about them when they were happening. A year and a half ago now his brother Leon died in her arms because his wife, Bets, couldn't bear it any longer, and when Walt came into that white room he didn't look at his brother. He looked at Sarah—pleaded with her, as if she were suddenly the God with answers her mother was always talking to—and he doesn't remember, because he wasn't there when it was happening, and even now, when he rambles on about himself and Leon making illegal whiskey in a cowshed—as if Fall River ever had a cowshed in the past hundred years, as if he ever drank illegal whiskey—it's so he won't remember anything he really remembers about a brother dying before him. Love, isn't it enough to describe? What for? Remember you holding me and me holding your dead brother and your eyes searching mine for some answer and me giving the only answer I knew how to give, which was to grip both of you, the living and the dead, and then, yes—you won't remember this because you weren't there when it was happening. I dropped him on the pillow and gripped you harder, and you dug your head into the nook of my shoulder and you wept no. Your brother who died too young because he went to Florida, state full of nothing but oranges and corpses; the man should have known, you said—I dropped him on the bed and gripped you and you wept no and you'll never remember.

Atlantic City

SARAH COMES HOME for lunch after her volunteer shift at the register in the hospital gift shop and finds Walt dead on the floor of their bedroom. He has been dead for at least two hours. His second and last heart attack, and from this one there was no turning back. The man turned fifty-nine only three months ago. This is September 1975. It has been a long morning, Friday mornings always are, and Sarah's feet hurt. She kneels beside his body and lifts his wrist to check for his pulse, even though she knows from looking at him. She knows. The way she knows it's morning through the thick drapes of a strange hotel room. The way she knows it's bad news by the way the phone rings mid-ring. Walt is dead. He is too young. He is dead. He is on his back with his suit pants on, sprawled, as though he went with fight. He clutches his wallet in his left hand. His teeth are still good and white. His shoes are polished. His tie is crooked, but tight and confident up to his big Adam's apple. He could be a toppled wax statue. He's wearing his watch. His hands are not clammy. He's wet himself. But still, he could be sleeping on the floor. He could be napping. He could have fallen, tripped, knocked his head against the telephone table and conked himself out. She rests an ear on his chest, not to listen for any movement of his dead exploded heart, but because she is suddenly so weary and he has been her fat pillow all these years. Though she doesn't want to sleep. She wants to rest awake. She sits up and takes off her shoes, then settles her head on his chest again, on his blue sea horses tie, on his sprawl. It isn't comfortable because of the angle, but she doesn't adjust. She remains still and listens to her own breathing. A bit quickened, but not hysterical, nothing even close to that. Other women, she thinks, would get hysterical. Run around moaning, dial telephone numbers furiously, shriek. The fools, she thinks, showy fools. Dingbats, Walt would call them. Dingbat chickens bawk-bawking. Walt, she thinks, too many sirloins at the Magoni's in Somerset. How many Howard Johnson hot dogs on a buttered bun? Ate, ate, ate like a happy hog across your life, and now I'm here. I could murder your head. You want to see tears? You want them to drop on your shirt so you can feel them on your skin? Didn't I tell you that time in Atlantic City that you waddled like an old man, that you needed to rest too much. You couldn't walk the boardwalk without getting so tired, and now look at you, Walt, can't even make it to work. That time in Atlantic City you laughed at me and said who the hell needs walking anyway. Bought us both another double cone. Pounded your chest and said, You got to live while you live. And that was all well and good for you. You don't have to come home to you like this. I have to come home to you. Walt. Atlantic City. Why Atlantic City now? That time in Atlantic City with Bernie and Nina Sadow. You on the beach. The only one of us who'd swim. Bernie had some kind of skin condition. Who knew with that man. It was always something. And

God, that Nina. Didn't stop talking to take a breath the three days we were down there. About what? You said you never heard so much nonsense since Saul Graboys talked you into buying his lemon El Dorado. But you swam, darling. Bernie with his skin condition and his chain of what? Check-cashing stores? Wasn't that it? Didn't Bernie Sadow own a chain of check-cashing stores in Newark? What a business to be in, no wonder he had a skin condition. You splashing and shouting at us. I stayed on the beach because I couldn't escape Nina's mouth. Bernie sitting there bundled up like it was February in Warsaw, and you, my fat brave knight, my tub-a-lard warrior, in the water splashing, throwing a tennis ball to those shouting boys. Those boys leaping out of the water like pale white porpoises. You swam with those boys. Why Atlantic City now? We haven't spoken to Bernie and Nina Sadow in how many years? You came back and shook your hair at us girls and said to Nina, Stop jabbering, woman. Stop! Come on, deadbeats, it's the Fourth of July in Atlantic City! Nina wanted to go back to the hotel and play cards. Bernie didn't want to do anything but tell strangers on the beach about all his ailments, that straw hat pulled down to his eyes, that huge coat, those big sunglasses. You said he looked like your Russian great-aunt, Aunt Portia Bertobobovitch. At least that got a smile out of Bernie, but Nina barely heard it over her own blather, except to say to me, Oh, your Walt's so hysterical. He's really got to be the most hysterical of all the husbands. Of all the husbands, she said, and for once, even though she went right back to complaining about the food at the hotel, for once that stupid woman had an ounce of wisdom. You said, Bernie, my big Polish babushka. And Bernie said, I thought you said I was Russian. Because Bernie had a sense of humor, which was more than you could say for Nina. And you said, Poland, Russia, it all looks the same to a Jew on the run, and Bernie, who was sensitive and serious on that point, didn't laugh, only said, Indeed. And later in the hotel you stood up on the bed with Q-tips sticking out your ears and mimicked Bernie's indeed. Indeed, indeed, indeed—who does he think he is, the queen's mother? Because Bernie was always finding new ways to remind people that he went to Harvard. But check cashing? Harvard College, Harvard Yard, and that's how he ended up making a living? Oh my lovely, my lovely, my lovely.

Providence

SARAH GOTTLIEB leans against the passenger-side door of Walt Kaplan's borrowed Ford Victoria. It's a shutter-thwacking Thursday morning in November 1938. Walt, clean-shaved, bandy-legged, stands on the sidewalk facing her, still not saying anything. So quiet now the only sound is the wind and the clack of the leaves somersaulting across bricks. Sarah is hefty, round-faced, and strong—mocking him with deviled eyes, tapping the toe of her high-heeled shoe on the running board of the car like a miniature hammer, her calf working, working. He's also chubby, closer to all-out fat than she is; he makes a face when he sucks in his belly so that he can button his pants. Now he's spreading his arms wide to form a huge bewildered Why? But still not speaking. Her face isn't budging, so what's the use of fighting back, of talking at her deaf ears. He grinds his teeth and involuntarily begs her name, mouths soundlessly, "Sarah." She doesn't bother to shake her head and certainly doesn't need to use her voice to say no again. Her face: Never, never, never, never, never. What do I care? Plead all day. It's still never, till hell freezes over and the goblins go ice-skating. Walt turns and looks at the pea-green house, sees the mother in the front window glaring. Which is worse, that ancient scowler or this hyena? Same face as the one in the window, only thicker and rosier. He wonders how a little flesh can make such a difference. That one in the window so far from beautiful he'd have to be chained and dragged to do the things that with this one he re-enacts in his head nightly, daily, afternoonly. He looks back at Sarah, who is now twirling a silver necklace around her pinkie. How could it have turned into this? She knows what we need to do. The paperwork's filed. And didn't she say three days ago that if she had to live in that putrid house another day she'd hang herself by the flagpole in front of Durfee High? Now he's ready, everything's ready, and here she is all done up and beautiful, lipstick and that hat, and all he can do is look daftly from her mouth to her knees, fat little knees he could eat without mustard. Because now it's an unbudgable no. Though it's no more than twenty degrees, he's sweating already in his new wool suit. Hasn't opened his trap since he pulled the car up to the house and already sweating like his undershirted father ranting around the store. Except he's here in broad daylight, on the sidewalk, pleading like the ignoramus she's convinced him he is. Sarah continues to tap her feet, her little doomsday clock ticking, ticking, sucking up his courage by the gallon. And there's nothing to say that he hasn't begged for with his eyes already. That if she wants to run, he'll run. That he's got a car. (Yes, it's his brother Leon's, but at least till Sunday night it's his.) Enough cash for the moment. A car and enough money. What else is there in this country? It's never been a question of going very far. He has a decent job, and though the mother's a lunatic, there are too many others in the family, too many friends; they can't leave for good. Simply going away for a few days to make it all legal. But that feverish tap-tap-tapping, that face taunting him. He feels the mother's eyes on the back of his head. Surrounded. Ambushed by women. Goddamnit, does he love this Sarah down to her shoes. God forgive him for wishing the mother a corpse already.

"Sare," he says, though he hadn't meant to. He'd meant to rehearse the final assault in his mind first, to get the sound right, somewhere in the gray between a bullyrag and a threat. But instead he only blurts, forcelessly, his voice octaves higher than he's ever heard it, "Sare—"

Only then it comes:

"Awright already."

Her voice, too, from somewhere other than her eyes and mouth, as though her throat rebelled before it could be hushed. A squeaked "Sare" answered by an irritated, but at the same time simple, unequivocal "Awright already." Have ever more glorious words been spoken by a woman? That evil crone in the house must notice something in the way Walt's shoulders go from clenched to juggly loose, because the next moment she's kicking open the front door and shrieking. Sarah very nearly doesn't have time to retrieve the little Samsonite she's hidden in the bushes beside the house. What the mother screams at them, who knows amid the slamming doors and the flush of the Ford's V-8? And their hyperventilating laughter, like two suddenly different people hurtling into that car. By the time the tiny shawled bundle of rage reaches the curb, Sarah and Walt are already sailing across Highland Avenue. To freedom, their first shared thought, as the car lunges forward, blurring houses, lawns, garages, a man raking leaves.

Left alone in front of the pea-green house, Frieda Gottlieb shouts at her staring neighbors, the frightened Portuguese

housewives peering sneakily out their kitchen windows. Forever convinced that still, after generations, not one of the en-
croachers knows a single word of English, Frieda barks, like
the schoolteacher she was a thousand years ago, "My daughter equals whore." She snarls, "Daughter, whore. In English
they mean the same thing."

In the car they head toward Providence, Rhode Island, where
the laws are easier. So long as you got a signed letter of con-
sent from the marriageable woman to the court three days
prior to the date of the proposed marriage, you could get a license in the morning, matrimony by afternoon. It was practically a money-back guarantee. You paid a little more than in
Massachusetts, but the speed made up for that. Sarah's practically asleep by the time they reach Tiverton. Her mouth is
open and she's breathing loudly, boisterously. Thirty-six miles
from Fall River to Providence overland. Tiverton to Providence eighteen miles. Nine-thirty now. License by 11:00,
married before 3:00 if the line's not too long. In Rhode Island
justices of the peace get paid by the marriage was what he'd
heard, so they get you out of there with no dilly and no dally.
After that, dinner at the Fore and Aft in Bristol. Then back to
Providence to the Wachman Hotel, where Artie Shaw always
stays when he's in town. And then *Arrivederci nature!* He
swoops a breath. *Hasta luego,* woods by the Watupa! *Ciao,*
blankets and trees! A bed, a bed, a bed, a bed, a bed, a bed, a
bed, a bed, a bed. A gust jolts them and the car swoons. Sarah
opens her eyes and murmurs, "Stop kidnapping me, Walt.
You have no right to kidnap." He watches her pull her heels
off and place her feet, feet as big as his, on the dash. She
yawns and droops her head again.

He thinks, The only bad thing about this is the secrecy. Of

course he'd told Leon everything. In order to get the car and the days off from the store, he'd had to. This meant that Bets knew everything, too. But both Leon and Bets knew they weren't to let anything out until Walt and Sarah got back from Rhode Island legitimate. Which meant the same thing in Massachusetts as it did in Rhode Island, because of the full faith and credit clause of the United States Constitution. Since he was going to have a wife instead of college, he was going to have to teach himself things. A marriage in Rhode Island's a marriage in Massachusetts, and so on and so forth. But more important than the paper they'd bring home was getting the green light from Sarah to tell everybody. This was her show—she was the one with that mother. The Kaplans, upstarts, were supposed to feel lucky Sarah was allowing Walt into their fold, who cared how. Because Frieda Gottlieb, of course, was a different kettle of fish; her money was older. She had a lot less of it, but that didn't matter. She might be locked away in that horrible green house in a neighborhood already gone to pot, but goddamnit it, her money was older, two generations older. The whole family, even the gang of pucker-faced cousins who talked like they were from England, make Walt squirm. And that Albert, always singing to himself, growing a full mustache at fifteen—even her little brother makes him nervous. The only one he likes is the dead father in the front hall picture, the one they all still talk to, good morning and good night, as if he's still among the living. But that mother . . . a snake with hair and legs.

He dismisses them all from his mind and rubs the leather on the side of the door, whistles quietly. Nineteen years old and he doesn't feel particularly old. But he doesn't feel that young anymore either. It's whole that he feels. More complete than yesterday. Yesterday, a day of trying on suits, shoes, ducking out of work early. Sarah's hand rests on the seat near his knee and he reaches for her wrist but doesn't touch it. Feet as big as his, but hands and wrists so small. Her wrists the daintiest thing about a girl not so dainty. He allows himself this moment where she can't chastise him. "You aren't marrying a ballerina," she'd say if she noticed him admiring her wrists, which would mean more than the obvious. It would also mean he wasn't marrying Bets, who used to dance ballet. Bets so light and tiny. Sometimes Leon carried her around on his palm like a waiter serving drinks. And yes, sometimes he does think about his sister-in-law's legs, the way she leaps when she walks, the way she closes her knees together when she sits, splaying her little bird feet out, but that's different, different.

Frieda Gottlieb tightens the shawl around her head by yanking on the ends. She stands in the front hall and looks at herself in the mirror and thinks of the ways Isadore went wrong with Sarah. The worst by far being that he took her to work with him. Let her play in the factory like a dirty-kneed Irish brat. Why did he raise her like she was a boy when he had a boy already? Grown man playing games with his daughter in a factory full of men and anybody has to ask where she went wrong? But wasn't she a beautiful baby, all cheeks, big pouches drooping? Frieda examines her own face, not wrinkled so much as pressed in, as though her features are retreating into her head. The girl's eighteen! Didn't I love you, Poo? I didn't play hide-and-seek with you and the grubby men who wanted to take you out in the field behind the factory and do unspeakables, but didn't I love you? Frieda looks at herself, but she talks now to Isadore, whose picture, as always, lurks behind her, lording the front hall as he never did in life. Always more court jester than king, and maybe if he'd taken his own life more seriously for half a second, *she* wouldn't be out there. Frieda listens to the slow creak of life as Albert begins his wake-up routine upstairs. Her late-sleeping son. So oblivious to anything that goes on in this house. Your sister's run away for good today. Huh? What, Ma? Whose runnin' where? She listens to Albert in the bathroom, the pipes groaning and thwacking throughout the house, the plumbing another reminder of Isadore's ineptitude. My daughter the slut with the little white suitcase her father gave her. Perhaps he knew how she was going to use it one day. Albert drops a glass on the bathroom floor. Yells, "Damnit! Ma!"

And she will not crawl back here no matter what monstrous else she's carrying besides that suitcase.

Frieda looks at her face and touches her forehead as if to mark her own words. That's what's for certain. Banished. She can drown in her own stew out there, never here. Frieda goes to the kitchen for a broom and dustbin. Just before her face leaves the mirror, she sees those jowls, how they sagged off that beautiful child like popped balloons.

After he finds a space on Benefit Street behind the courthouse, Walt gently shakes her awake. Sarah opens her eyes slowly and realizes the car has stopped, that it's happening. For the first time all day her eyes betray that she's frightened. She has been since the moment she woke up and began furiously packing the suitcase, but she wasn't foolish enough to let Walt know. She was well aware what impact her fear would have on his resolve. Walt so skittish. Puffs his chest like such a big man, but when it comes down to it, he's scared of anything and everybody, especially her mother, who will twist her hands together for how long after this escape? Escape! As if this even resembled one. If what they were doing was escaping, they were like a couple of convicts breaking out and then stopping for coffee across the street from the prison. They weren't forty miles from Fall River. After three nights in a hotel (of all of it, the news that they'd stayed in a hotel would torture her mother the most), they'd go home. To a little place he found on Weetamoe, the top half of a house that at least, thank God, wasn't green. It was fading yellow, nearly white in the sun. Walt would take a risk only so far. But it made sense, didn't it? His job. Our friends. *But couldn't we have gone and done this out of New England?* So the fear in her eyes isn't of her mother's wrath, which can take a flying leap for all she cares. Let her yowl her head off. Let her rot in that house, with the neighbors hiding under their kitchen tables.

No, what Sarah's afraid of is Monday afternoon, of being alone in that little furnished place on Weetamoe on Monday afternoon, of staring out the window at the corner. She sees herself watching some Italian kid jumping rope in the street. A little girl in a brown dress with big buttons that flops as she leaps. The girl, clean-faced but dirty all over, doesn't see her, and wouldn't think much if she had. Just another lady staring out the window like bored ladies do. But what choice do I have really? And aren't I getting out of that house? Weetamoe's only ten blocks up the hill from Robeson, but isn't there a continent in those ten blocks? From her face, yes. Which is all that counts, though of course she also knows that a mother's silent judgment reaches you wherever you are. That'd be true if she ran to Rio de Janeiro.

Walt doesn't notice the glaze of fear in her eyes. He's straightening his tie and tucking in his shirt as best he can while he's still sitting in the driver's seat.

"All right, banana," he says. "Good sleep?"

She doesn't say anything, just looks at him, curious at how someone can just plow along, unbogged. Not even fathoming what this is about, and it's so obvious. Nostrils in a book his whole life, like her yeshiva-boy cousin Harry. Maybe reading shrinks Walt's brain. She's almost envious, and for a second she permits herself to be genuinely pleased. But she resists the urge to say something nice to him and slips on her shoes. She gets out of the car and takes in the huge red-brick courthouse, which according to Walt is famous in Providence because it dates back to the time of Roger Williams. Roger Williams, she thinks, another one who fled Massachusetts for postage-stamp Rhode Island. But at least *he* never got back in his canoe and went home to Monday morning. She stands on tiptoe and talks to Walt over the roof of the car.

"I wasn't going to do this, you know."

"Oh." Walt lolls his head on the edge of the top of the car and watches her. He's on the verge of smiling outright, but he's unwilling to risk it.

"I only put my suitcase in the bushes in case I capitulated."

He perks his head up. "So you capitulated?" Now he laughs. "Oh, Sare, I didn't think you had it—"

"I didn't say I did."

"Oh."

"I just changed my mind. *You* certainly didn't convince me of anything. And you aren't rescuing me either, so put your white horse back in the stable."

"You're as booby a meshuggeneh as your mother."

She sniggers, but doesn't say anything. Walt walks around the car and takes hold of her arms. She thrusts her head away, dramatically, like a girl in the movies who really wants to be kissed but doesn't want to show it, except that Sarah doesn't want to be kissed. Right now she doesn't even want to look at him for fear that he will see what her joy looks like. Because even though she's a little woozy now, it's there, and it's disgusting. Smack on her face in Rhode Island. He'll see, and then he'll kill himself trying to make it so she feels this way for three days straight. And God forbid longer. Which would not only be impossible, it would make her berserk. So to rid herself of joy, she imagines what's to come. She thinks of the calculations. Hmmm, let's see, if the baby was born in May, hmmmm, well, there's November, December, January, February, March, hmmm . . . But even that's a hell of a lot better than being invisible, and she thinks again of that girl skipping rope in the street, not even bothering to look up at the lady in the window. And she watches herself, Sarah, ram her fist through the glass to get that little snot's attention.

"You want to walk around the block? Huh? My cauliflower? My eggplant, my Sallygirl? Wake up a little more?"

She doesn't answer, only jerks from his grip and marches toward the looming steps. Walt, without hesitation, hustles into line behind her, smoothing his suit with trembling hands. She's a plump, high-heeled Black Jack Pershing in a blue hat with white frills, and he's a grinning doughboy who'd follow her into any slaughter without a second thought, mortar fire bursting, come what may.

4.

THE WATERS

By God we'll love each other or die trying.

—Sherwood Anderson,
"Song of the Soul of Chicago,"
from *Mid-American Chants*

Michigan City, Indiana

A WHITE-BORDERED black-and-white photograph of my grandfather and my father looking out at Lake Michigan. The picture was taken in Michigan City, Indiana, in the late 1940s. My grandfather and my father are visible from behind. There is no mistaking the shape of my grandfather. He is 5'7", bold, forward, and squat. The muscles in his shoulders are bunched up so that his neck and his shoulders meet as one, like the gentle slope at the bottom of a mountain. He is pointing at the lake. With his other hand he is holding my father's hand. My father is wearing a fedora that is too big for his head.

My grandfather is telling my father about the lake, about how many miles it is from north to south, east to west, about how ferocious it can be, about the ships it has swallowed. He is telling my father about the towns with Indian names along the Michigan and Wisconsin coasts. Muskegon, Manistee, Sheboygan, Mantiwoc. A place called Fort Michilimackinac, where the British vanquished the French in 1761. My father says nothing. When my grandfather was gone in the war, my father used to draw pictures of him riding on his ship. Pictures with crayon captions like YOU KILLER JAPS BEWARE

MY DAD!!! But now that my grandfather has returned, my father is afraid of him, of his shouting confidence, of the attacking way he handles his fork at the dinner table. And my father knows that the war didn't make my grandfather this way. He remembers it was this way before, too. He'd hoped with all his pictures and all his praying that the war would either change his father or kill him. Neither has happened. And he is ten years old and looking out into the glare of the summer lake, and although my grandfather's voice is soft and playful, the hand that holds my father's is a wrench that slowly tightens around his aching fingers. The boy stares out at the vast and tries to see what his father sees.

The Raft

M Y GRANDFATHER, who lost his short-term memory sometime during the first Eisenhower administration, calls me into his study because he wants to tell me the story he's never told anybody before, again. My grandmother, from her perch at her dressing table, with the oval mirror circled by little bulbs I used to love to unscrew, shouts, "Oh, for God's sake, Seymour. We're meeting the Dewoskins at Twin Orchard at seven-thirty. Must you go back to the South Pacific?"

My grandfather slams the door and motions me to the chair in front of his desk. I'll be thirteen in two weeks. "There's something I want to tell you, son," he says. "Something I've never told anybody. You think you're ready? You think you've got the gumption?"

"I think so."

"Think so?"

"I know so, sir. I know I've got the gumption."

He sits down at his desk and stabs open an envelope with a gleaming letter opener in the shape of a miniature gold sword. "So you want to know?"

"Very much."

"Well then, stand up, sailor." My grandfather's study is carpeted with white shag. It feels woolly against my bare feet. I twist my toes in it. In the room there are also many cactuses. My grandfather often encourages me to touch their prickers to demonstrate how tough an old bird a plant can be. My grandfather captained a destroyer during World War II.

"It was late," he says. "There was a knock on my state-room door. I leaped up. In those days I slept in uniform—shoes, too." My grandfather smiles. His face is so perfectly round that his smile looks like a gash in a basketball. I smile back.

"Don't smile," he says. "Just because I'm smiling, don't assume I couldn't kill you right now. Know that about a man."

"Oh, Seymour, *my God,*" my grandmother says through the door. "Anyway, isn't he supposed to be at camp? Call his mother."

He looks at me and roars at the door, "Another word out of you, ensign, and I'll have you thrown in the brig, and you won't see Beanie Dewoskin till V-J Day."

"I'll make coffee," my grandmother says.

"It was late," I say. "There was a knock."

"Two knocks," he says. "And by the time he raised his knuckle for the third, I'd opened the door. 'A message from the watch, sir. A boat, sir, three miles due north. Very small, sir. Could be an enemy boat, sir; then again, it might not be. Hard to tell, sir.' I told the boy to can it. Some messengers don't know when to take a breath and let you think. They think if you aren't saying anything, you want to hear more, which is never true. Remember that. I went up to the bridge. 'Wait,' I told them. 'Wait till we can see it. And ready the torpedoes,' I told them, or something like that, I forget the lingo."

157 // *The Raft*

"The torpedoes?" I say.

"Yes," he says. "The torpedoes. I couldn't make it out, but the chance that it wasn't a hostile boat was slim. You see what I'm driving at?"

"I do, sir."

"No, you don't, sailor."

"No, I don't," I say. "Don't at all."

"We'd been warned in a communiqué from the admiral to be on high alert for kamikaze flotillas. Do you have any idea what a kamikaze flotilla is?"

"Basically," I say, "it hits the side of your boat, and whango."

"You being smart with me? You think this isn't life and death we're talking about here?"

"Sorry, sir."

"So I waited. It took about a half hour on auxiliary power for us to get within a quarter mile of the thing—then I could see it with the search."

My grandfather pauses, opens his right-hand desk drawer, where he keeps a safety-locked pistol and a stack of pornographic comic books. They are strange books. In the cartoons men with long penises with hats on the ends of them and hair growing up the sides, so that to me they look like pickles, chase women with their skirts raised over their heads and tattoos on their asses that say things like *Uncle Sam's my daddy* and *I never kissed a Kaiser.* He whacks the drawer shut and brings his hands together in front of his face, moves his thumbs around as if he's getting ready either to pray or to thumb-wrestle. "Japs," he says. "Naked Japs on a raft. A raftload of naked Jap sailors. Today the bleedyhearts would probably call them refugees, but back then we didn't call them anything but Japs. Looked like they'd been floating for days. They turned their backs to the light, so all we could see were their backsides, skin and bone fighting it out and the bone winning hands down."

I step back. I want to sit down, but I don't. He stands and leans over his desk, examines my face. Then he points at the door, murmurs, "Bernice doesn't know." On a phone-message pad he scrawls, BLEW IT UP in capital letters. Whispers, "*I gave the order.*" He comes around the desk and motions to his closet. "We can talk in there," he says, and I follow him into his warren of suits. My grandfather long ago moved all his clothes out of my grandmother's packed-to-the-gills closets. He leaves the light off. In the crack of sun beneath the door I can see my grandfather's shoes and white socks. He's wearing shorts. He'd been practicing his putting in the driveway.

"At ease, sailor," he says, and I kneel down amid the suits and dangling ties and belts. And I see now that it's not how many times you hear a story but where you hear it that matters. I've heard this before, but this is the first time I've been in a closet alone with my grandfather.

"Why?" I say. "Why, if you knew it wasn't—"

"Why?" he says, not like he's repeating my question but as if he really doesn't know. He sighs. Then, still whispering even though we're in the closet, he says, "Some men would lie to you. They'd say it's war. I won't lie to you. It had zero to do with war and everything to do with the uniform I was wearing. Because my job was to make decisions. Besides, what the hell would I have done with a boatload of naked Japanese? There was a war on."

"But you just said—"

"Listen, my job. Just because men like me made the world safe for men like your father to be cowards doesn't mean you won't ever blow up any civilians. Because you will. I do it once a week at the bank." He places a stumpy, powerful hand on my shoulder. *"Comprende?"*

"Never," I breathe. "Good," he says, and we are standing in the dark and looking at each other, and the story is the same and different—like last time, except this time his tears come so fast they're like lather. He blows his nose into his hand. I reach and offer him the sleeve of one of his suit jackets. "I'll let myself out," he says, and leaves me in the confessional, closing the door behind him.

This time I don't imagine anything, not even a hand that feels like a fish yanking my ankle. Another door opens. "Seymour? Seymour?" my grandmother says. "Where's the kid?"

The House on Lunt Avenue

IT IS EARLY Monday morning on Lunt Avenue, Roger's Park, Chicago. November 1954. Seymour Burman shouts at his son Philip, the boy who will become my father. It is ten before seven and Seymour's anger smells of Scotch. Philip is eighteen and has flunked out of the University of Illinois. He lies on his old bed with a pillow over his face. The room stinks of filthy socks. Seymour paces the sliver of room not taken up by the bed. The floor creaks beneath the frayed carpet, which was once green but is now the stagnant brown of the puddles that lie near the sewers along Lunt Avenue waiting to be frozen by December. Philip lifts the pillow from his face and yawns.

"And tomorrow?" Seymour lifts a big cordovan leather shoe and stamps it for emphasis. It doesn't resound. *This house.* In a part of his brain not currently outraged by his slothful son, he decides, once and for all, the time has come to buy a place in the north suburbs.

"Don't you have to go to work?" Philip says.

"You're a miserable lazy."

Philip props himself against the headboard. "Tomorrow. For Christ sake, I said tomorrow."

"You think it's all free? Is that what?"

"What?"

Seymour flaps his arms. "This! This!"

Philip rolls his eyes and looks out the window. Even on this rare, bright November morning, the sunlight hardly creeps into the room because the house next door is so close, a proximity that used to be this room's single consolation. Millie Finkle's bedroom window is no more than ten feet away. Millie was in the class ahead of him at Sullivan and mostly ignored him. There were nights, though, when he caught her figure against the light, behind the pulled shade. But Millie is gone now, an Alpha Something Phi at Wisconsin, and already engaged to a darling handsome boy studying law at Northwestern. This information courtesy of Mrs. Finkle, whispering in his mother's ear at the market. So now the possibility across the way is back to being a window, and Philip is home again, a disgrace to the family.

"This is unacceptable!" Seymour booms.

"Give it a rest."

"You think I joke. I'll call a locksmith." He bolts from the room, pounds down the stairs—for a stocky man, he moves fast—and grabs his fur hat off the front hall table. The house shakes after the slam of the front door, then is calm. Philip shuts his eyes and in a moment is nearly asleep, thinking not of Millie but of where she lives now. Soft bodies in an enormous foggy bathroom. White cream on faces, scurrying legs.

In pajama bottoms and no shirt, Philip wanders the house. His little sister, Esther, must be at school. His mother is probably teaching dance. The house stands, silent and empty, except for his grandmother, who never leaves the guest room anyway. He stops by the door and listens to her cranky breathing. She's awake. Grandma Rachel breathes like that, as if she's asleep, even when she's not, even while she sits and stares at nothing. She'll never die. He doesn't knock.

There's a note from his mother on the kitchen table. (Four dollars is enclosed.) "Two roast beef sandwiches in the fridge. In wax paper, behind the tomato juice. Have a wonderful day! Ignore the Admiral. He's just letting out hot air. If he doesn't exhale, he'll explode all over. He does love you. By the way, they're hiring at Goldy's, so you might be able to get your old job back. Hint. Hint. Kisses."

Bernice stands before the mirror in the ballet studio above Al Fonroy's Shirts and Slacks on Touy Avenue. Sweat pours down her neck and chest, soaking the front of her leotard. Her mind is on nothing but her flexibility and the power of her own legs. She stretches in the mirrors, which double her image to infinity. There's nothing else in the world but this movement. Even at this small-time level. Yes, yes, there was a time when bigger was possible. Before Seymour, the children, and the war. This Seymour can't take away. The great Lincoln Kirstein himself watched her dance in a Ruth Page production of *Frankie and Johnny*. And after the show—she remembers this often—while the Russian girls were tittering a mile a minute, he approached her without introduction (his huge forehead gleaming) and said, simply, "Why not come to New York? I've started a school." And she almost went. Even now visions of dancing "Morning, Noon, and Night" at the Capitol Theatre invade her dreams. She extends her arms, slides, runs a step, a *grande fouetté* right, then half-turns. Pauses, opens her legs wide, turns into a slow leap, and muffs a *tour jeté*. Lands, turns, slides, slides, shuffles left, and is about to leap again—

"Bernice?"

"Yes."

"Your son's here."

She grips the bar and raises her leg slowly. In the mirror she examines the thin wrinkles that are now etched below her eyes like tiny veins in a marble pillar.

Philip will learn. She knows this. He'll catch on. He'll go to work. They always do. And thank God. They couldn't possibly not work. What would we do with them? But this doesn't mean the need won't go on. Her men. Esther has never had this. Always an independent young thing. Esther, who used to love getting lost in the vast shoe section of Marshall Field's, who would try on big men's shoes and waddle around and quack at anyone who'd listen to her. Her daughter still thinks this life's not a defeat. But the men have always been different. Even Seymour, for all his bluster, couldn't find the ears in his head if she wasn't there to tell him where they were. And no matter how far they stray, they always return, guilty smiles spread across their mouths, begging for forgiveness, eyes to the floor. Seymour came back from the war a hero with his tail between his legs. And Philip's the same. He'll pull himself together. But like his father, there's something missing in him, not an essential thing, at least not to Seymour. Warmth, some courage, even love surface in both of them from time to time. Still, something's not there. She slides again, leaps, and tries another *tour jeté,* this one a little better. The missing thing, she knows the moment she lands, so easy. You don't need talent, nothing. Only grace. The room begins to fill with other dancers. Bernice mops her neck with a towel.

"Tell him I'm teaching. Tell him my purse is on the bench in the backroom."

* * *

Tuesday morning, and the tweed coat doesn't fit and smells of Pall Malls. Philip Burman looks like a kid playing dress-up. The coat is left over from his high-school days, and it didn't fit well even then. A hand-me-down from his Uncle Wallace. Wallace was ten years younger than Seymour, closer in age to his nephew than to his brother. The story goes that he laughed a lot—out loud—deep belly laughs that made the rest of the family nervous. The other legend is that it wasn't just a heart attack that dropped Wallace dead at thirty-eight, but also the stormy intensity of my grandfather to excel, to expand, to go public. Wallace was famous for failing. He didn't pay attention to unpaid balances. He neglected details, forgot appointments, always ran late. He sired only daughters.

On the El, Philip tugs his sleeves in an attempt to stretch the coat's arms. The knot under his chin is excruciatingly tight, but he knows if he loosens his tie his father will notice right away. Today he will suffer it. The other people on the subway stare straight ahead or out the window at the tar-paper roofs of stores and the back porches of rambling tenements. Their bundled shoulders jolt with every lurch of the train.

At the office Philip examines claims. He makes check marks. His job is to search for inconsistencies. In the numbers, in the descriptions of the accidents, in the words of his father, which liar did what to the other liar? He shuffles his feet under his table. The office is cold, and he bounces his legs to keep his feet warm. The place is so silent that the flap of the turning of papers gets on his nerves. Washing out the fat drawer at Goldy's beat this. Fred and Myron yammering about the price of hog whatevers and beans.

The one bright spot is his father's secretary. Her name is Shirl. Not Shirley. She's already corrected him twice. "Only my mother calls me Shirley and she lives in Toledo." She's got on a thin print dress that is too short and summery for the weather. She's got plump cheeks and sighs a lot.

Behind Shirl, beyond the closed office door, Seymour sits at his desk, a paperweight gripped in his hand. Just before lunch he often daydreams about the war. Today, in a starchy uniform and creased leather-brimmed hat, he struts the bridge. The captain. Of all the guys on the ship, there's only one guy who's captain. He thinks about shaking Jackie Cooper's hand at Nouméa, New Caledonia. How many men can say they held Jackie Cooper's sweaty palm in theirs?

Seymour's lackey, a very tall, timid, small-eyed man named Roger Craigson, has the office to the right of his boss. Craigson's door is open. It's Craigson who gives Philip work. He approaches Philip's little table, blinking profusely, forcing a smile.

"Howz it?"

"I guess all right. I found some inconsistent things."

"Excellent. Let's have a look at your effort." Much is not said. Craigson is wary of the boss's kid. Craigson had a wife once, but she ran, and now he wears this humiliation in the smile that juts out both edges of his mouth like twin scars. He's prepared for any kind of insult—he's endured them all—and he looks at Philip and waits for him to say something snide. But Philip says nothing, just points to what he's found and waits for Craigson to leave so he can stare more at Shirl's breasts, which project from her chest like the prows of attacking ships. She types like a banshee. The letters whack the paper as if she's punching a bag.

Seymour's door bangs open. "I'll be at the Berghoff," he

says. Shirl nods and looks curiously at Philip, who—she'd noticed—looked down immediately at the sight of his father.

"I just wanted to talk to you," Philip says. "Outside the office." The bartender clinks glasses, hums a silent song to himself. He's shrivel-faced and small, so tiny only his head bobs
above the bar, like a begging child. He looks at my father and
sucks his cheeks. The place is called the Charlie Boo's: nothing more than a cramped narrow room, hardly more than the
bar itself, some stools and green and brown bottles in front of
a mirror. A jukebox is jammed against the far wall. There's
one guy at the end who looks as if he's counting his fingers,
over and over.

It is Thursday evening, four blocks from the office. Philip
has followed Shirl.

"Look. I don't want to be harsh, but you're a kid. Not only
are you a kid, but you're the honcho's kid."

"I just wanted to talk to you. Without Craigson's eyes."

Shirl sighs and glances at herself in the mirror, nudges her
hair. "Don't think about him. He's a dopey. Worry about the
honcho." She looks at the door. "Look, anyway, I'm waiting
for somebody."

Philip, his hands in his lap, rubs his thumbs together. "I'll
wait with you until your friend comes," he says.

"Uy yuy yuy," she says, warming to him. She orders two
beers from the little bartender.

The bartender looks doubtfully at Philip and winks at
Shirl.

"The kid trailed me."

"You want me to take him by the ear?"

"I'm twenty-five," Philip says, and puts a ten-dollar bill on
the table.

"I'm Adlai Stevenson," the bartender says, and places two glasses before them.

"Thank you, Boo Bear," Shirl says. She has a slight double chin, a second layer of skin softly rounds and dips below her jaw. She turns to Philip. "So you flunked out of school and now you're working for Daddy."

"Not for long."

"What are you going to do?"

"I don't know. Something else."

"Does the big guy know?"

"Screw him," Philip says. "It doesn't matter. I'm getting my own place. And a different job. So—" Shirl laughs and leans into the bar, tips over a glass with her elbow. A foamy stream nearly flows over the bar, but Philip blocks it with his sleeve before it has a chance to drop and spill all over her dress.

Shirl rattles the bar. Says, "What about a little whiskey for the babe in the woods?"

She lives on the third floor of a walk-up on North Pratt. They get off the El and walk along streets lined with dirty plowed snow that looks like piled ash. Now bundled in Wallace's beer-stained coat, Shirl marches ahead. Philip follows in shirtsleeves, quietly shivering, fearful of saying the wrong thing and being sent home. It is after midnight and they've been drinking for hours. Across the street from Shirl's building is a construction site, a large pit ringed by earth-moving machines that look to Philip like giant sleeping dinosaurs. Shirl flings open the lobby door. He watches her bare red ankles as she tromps up the stairs.

Shirl unlocks her door and leads him into a black hall. She turns on the light. "This is where I live," she says. He blinks, and through the purple light in his eyes he sees a green couch and a metal card table. She flicks the light off. "You saw it. There it was." She leads him, clackety-clacking, through a dark room to a bed twice the size of the one in his own room. She pushes him onto to it, kisses him, then rolls over and pulls her dress over her head. He places his hands on Shirl's coarse bra and shuts his eyes. The bed twirls. Shirl unbuttons his shirt, kisses him again, and bites his lip with a pointy incisor. He grabs her shoulders and squeezes. His feet begin to thaw.

"I have a cat," she says.

Philip murmurs that he hates cats.

"You won't hate Theresa. Nobody hates Theresa." Her movements are quicker now, more abrupt, as though she wants to settle whatever this night's going to turn into before she is too exhausted to move anymore. She yanks his shoes off and throws them across the room. She unzips his pants, pulls the cuffs, and slides them off. Scrunches next to him. "Okay," she says, and licks his ear. "Let's get this circus under way."

"You smell like peaches," he whispers.

"Nice. That's nice," Shirl says, and pulls him toward her. Then she scuttles atop him and jams her breasts into his chest. He squirms. There's some wet back-and-forthing, but other than that, he feels nothing but the somersault of the room. Shirl's legs wiggle. She laughs and flounces.

In the morning it takes him a few panicked moments to figure out where he is. That cat glares at him from the floor. She's made a nest out of Wallace's coat. The room has no pictures. There is only this cat. Shirl's knee digs into his thigh.

Her mouth is open and her breath is loud and windy. When he gets out of bed, Shirl rolls over but doesn't wake up. Philip parts the curtains and looks out the window as he buttons his shirt. It's begun to snow. Tiny flecks pelt the window and turn to water, ride down the pane in streaks.

He watches Shirl and is shocked by the blurry memory that he'd reached for her in the night, in his stupor, and found her drawn away, huddled, wedged to the wall. He'd reached for her. He'd clawed across the sheets for her. It makes him think of his sister, who used to sneak into his room in the middle of the night and sleep under his bed. In the morning he'd wake up to a little hand reaching up, as if from the dead, twisting the skin of his arm. How he used to scream for his mother, and she'd stand in his room and say, "Esther only just adores you." He looks at Shirl's muddle of hair across the pillow. I clawed across the sheets for you. He leaves the coat to the cat.

In half an hour Shirl will wake up alone and dress and return to work, where she will type and file and endure Seymour's gruff another day. Over lunch she will tell her girlfriend Irene from the accountant's office down the hall about the honcho's kid. Young, sort of fumbly, shadowed me down to Charlie Boo's.

But Philip won't show up for work today. He won't go home to Lunt Avenue or to his mother, either. Instead, he will roam. Probably not beyond Peterson to the south, or Howard to the north, but for a while at least my father, in shirtsleeves, will roam the slush-brown sidewalks of this city he will never leave.

Daughters

WHATEVER HAPPENED, it happened the night of April 20, 1960, the night Bunny Hirsh hosted an extravaganza to celebrate her husband Franklin's two decades in business. The wow years, as he called them. He'd turned a storefront Ashland Avenue dry-goods shop into an empire that stretched the Midwest vertically. *Both Dakotas to Cairo, Illinois . . . People Trust Hirsh Drugs.* My grandmother claims it was the grandest hoopla ever thrown in a private house. *And the house!* One of those American-made castles on the lake side of Sheridan Road, the ones that make you slow down and gawk, amazed that anybody could be so ostentatious in such a cold climate. Theirs was a three-floor Italian palazzo with a tower, the roof of which was pink and looked like an upside-down sugar cone. "Garish," my grandmother said. "Very *very* garish." Both Illinois senators made appearances, along with a babbling cackle of congressmen. Sid Luckman, the old Jewish quarterback, the man everyone wanted their sons to grow up to be, sauntered in with his— *shhhhhhhhhhhh*—half-black fourth wife. Mayor Daley was there, drinking cranberry juice and rigorously cleaning his ears with his fingers. Suburbia made him fidgety. My grandmother was so concerned about her hair for the party that she went back to the beauty shop twice to have her wave reset. ("Really, I was never so close to leaving Chad in my entire life.") That night the front hallway was decorated with irises and wild lilies imported, people said, from Baha, California, that morning. And there was Paula. Paula Hirsh had flown in from Colgate for the weekend. She was twenty. A startling redhead. Her hair was so unusually orange that people had often wondered who delivered this girl to Bunny and Franklin's doorstep in a basket. Paula looked more like an Irish princess ("If there ever was such a thing," my grandmother said) than the daughter of rumpled, floppy-breasted Franklin, a man who always stood crouched like the army boxer he'd once been. By no stretch of anyone's imagination was he handsome. Bunny, of course, had been beautiful once, but according to my grandmother, she'd gotten considerably more severe and horsy-looking over the years. Yet their daughter, the ravishing anomaly, glided across the marble tile floors that night proud of her father's money and her mother's way with a party. Paula was not, and had never been known to be, a rebellious girl. Guests remembered her greeting them at the door that night as if she were her mother's twin. She welcomed people with the same flutter. *Mrs. Katzenbaum! You could be his daughter! Come in, come in, both of you* . . . She danced, laughed, whispered gossip with the other college girls, including my Aunt Esther. She also drank, ate chocolates, and, as her mother had demanded, circulated.

The story goes roughly like this: At one point, not very late in the party, Paula Hirsh spilled punch on her dress. She'd been in the middle of a conversation with a man who was soon to become famous in the papers. An unknown, at least to Bunny's set; it came out later that he hadn't been invited. His name was Isaac Persky and he was the son of a pawnbroker from Hyde Park. His father still talked Yiddish. "How that boy got into that party," my grandmother said, "God only knows." Later that night, after they arrested him, Persky told police that after the spill Paula excused herself with a playful toss of her head ("How clumsy, be right back"). He said he gave way and watched her disappear into the kitchen, and that, Isaac Persky swore, was the last he saw of her.

"On Fargo Avenue," my grandmother said. "I was Bernie Shlansky and she was Bunny Eisendrath. Bernie and Bunny. Her real name was Muriel, but her father called her Bunny because she never stopped moving, even in her sleep. The girl wore her favorite rubber boots to bed. We danced together at the Chicago Theater on the northside, the Tivoli on the southside, and McVicker's in the middle. For two years, on school vacations, we traveled with Benny Meroff and his orchestra as part of his dancing girls. I never had a sister. My head on the El tracks for her would have been nothing. She was under the table when Benny Meroff himself stole a kiss from me—God knows why; I was the homely one, especially with my old nose. Anyway, Bunny tried to protect me, even though I didn't want protection. I liked it. Benny Meroff's slippery lips. But there she was, leaping up from under the table shouting *Fire! fire! fire!* like a lunatic. She was there the night I pranced onstage at the Oriental without my tights. And she was a hell of lot better showgirl than I was. Nobody shimmied like her. Could she have gone to New York? Absolutely. But who wanted that? We didn't want to be discovered. We wanted to be wives in Chicago. (Of course, if anybody at the time had told me the truth about that pursuit . . . but that's neither here nor there anymore.) We got married, had children, daughters. Her husband got richer than mine. God knows, you didn't need to hire an accountant to figure that out. Man got rich as Croesus selling Kaopectate. But I had Esther, and Esther was Esther. Such a doll, nobody'd stop talking about her. A genius at everything she touched. Ballet, piano, violins, the balance beam, even school. Seymour taught her how to shoot, and she won prizes doing that. And Paula Hirsh was Paula Hirsh. Quieter than Esther (but who wasn't?), much less the little bulldozer. When they were girls, Esther used to boss Paula around. Make her walk the dog while she sat on the grass in bare feet singing bathroom songs. Things like that. Girl so unlike her mother, and it drove Bunny daffy. Finally they sent her away to prep school near Boston. Bunny thought maybe Illinois was the problem. I hardly saw Paula in those years except when she came home for school vacations. But even then she was still so shy, hiding behind that strange red hair, following you with her eyes but not saying one word. I always had the feeling she was somewhere else when her mother was rattling on. You know, Bunny could talk a storm to sleep and not say a single thing worth remembering. I remember—not so long before— Paula had told her she decided to major in botany at college. God, did that have Bunny in hysterics. Her shouting, 'My only daughter wants to be a florist!' But at the party, that *party of parties,* she couldn't have been more different, and Bunny beamed. *Look, Bernice, the girl's escaped herself.* It was there in Bunny's eyes as she kissed me and pulled me into the house that night. *Look at her! Look at my daughter!* And then, Lord knows, it happened.

At around 11:30, a guest happened to be looking out a window in Franklin's den at the back, dark part of the house. A snooper, my grandmother said, the kind who creeps around the dark outskirts of a party and takes inventory of your silver, checks the labels under your cushions. She was the wife of one of Franklin's lawyers, and she was looking out the back windows trying to estimate how much land Franklin owned between the house and the lake. She noticed a shadow in the empty pool.

"The orchestra was playing 'Londonderry Air' and just like that they cut off. But even so, it got louder, so much louder after the band stopped. *So much much louder.*"

She was naked when they found her. This fact led to great speculation in the Chicago papers, involving, as a matter of course, the hired help of the caterer (especially two black waiters whose pictures were run in the *Trib*) and the pawnbroker's son, the infamous party-crasher, who, it was said, might have been driven wretched and murderous by the sight of what he could never have. (What the black waiters might have wanted with Paula Hirsh, nobody would say out loud.) It was also reported that Paula's third-floor bedroom window was open, her fingerprints on the window handle. Her dress was neatly folded on the bed. Water and baking soda had been rubbed into the stain. The only thing askew in the room was a lamp found smashed on the rug.

* * *

"Nobody ever had much of a clue. Such a soft-spoken girl. But did she have friends? A busload of them came from out East for the funeral. I'm telling you, a busload crying their eyes out."

Bunny Hirsh put her faith in the overturned lamp. "My daughter," she announced from behind a black veil to the friends gathered at the house after the funeral, "was attacked and pushed out her own window. No one will ever be safe in their own homes again." After the investigation dragged on for months, not a shred of new evidence was found. People started to say out loud what they hadn't had the courage to say before: that Paula Hirsh had knocked the lamp over herself when she climbed up on the sill. But still the questioning continued. ("They drove Persky's father out of business with all that suspicion," my grandmother huffed. "And the blacks, God only knows what hell it was for them.") Then people began to murmur that Franklin Hirsh had paid off the police in order to appease his now insane wife.

"All that red hair, but so so timid. Once, early on, her mother sent her away to camp to get her to talk more. A theater camp of some kind up in Michigan, near Charlevoix. Two weeks later the camp director wrote and told Bunny her daughter had a brilliant career ahead of her as a mime." My grandmother laughed. "It was a routine letter; I used to get things like it all the time for Esther. *Esther has a brilliant career ahead of her in tennis, Esther has a brilliant career ahead of her as a water-skier, a chef, a yeoman archer.* Bunny and I drove up to Michigan to rescue Paula that afternoon. *My daughter isn't going to be anybody's freak show.* And Paula, as if she had a premonition we were coming, had on all that white makeup when we stuffed her in the car—she couldn't have been more than nine or ten then. Bunny was so furious she couldn't speak. But Paula and I did. We sat in the back together and laughed as I wiped her face with Kleenex that Bunny kept tossing back to us like plucked flowers."

She stops on the narrow stairwell and listens to the trumpet, shoulders the wall in the dark, lingers to the slow murmur. The horn eases. She goes up again.

They were having tea on the patio. Bunny's chair faced away from the swimming pool. It was three months after Paula's death, July 1960. My grandmother had spent every morning with Bunny since the catastrophe, long after other friends went back to their lives and started whispering about how even in mourning Bunny Hirsh was a prima donna. But my grandmother remained her loyal lieutenant. My grandmother patted her head and stroked her neck and held her, absorbed Bunny's tears and her fury. For hours on end out there, she listened, stroked. But that morning my grandmother said something else. She told me she couldn't say exactly why she did it. But wasn't she grieving also? Wasn't Paula a daughter to her, too?

"We can't know them, really, even our own flesh. Even our own daughters, Bun. You could never have known."

Bunny Hirsh stood up and dropped her cup on the bricks —simply opened her hand and let it fall. She stood there with her fingers spread wide and faced the pool. Then she stalked into the house. A few moments later, while my grandmother was still kneeling and picking up the shards, her palm bleeding, the new maid came out and said Mrs. Hirsh was lying down and no longer felt well enough to entertain guests. *Guest?* She'd known Bunny five hundred years. They'd danced together. They'd both started at Miss Rucker's when they were six years old. How many numbers had they done together? The Piccadilly, Honor of Lady Elgin, the New Georgia Serenade, Iroquois Fire Dance, the Pica Pica, Sailor's Hornpipe.

The palazzo has long been sold off, remodeled, subdivided into apartments. The trim's been repainted an even brighter pink than it was in Franklin's time. There's a circular drive-way now. The pool's been filled in. It's impossible to know it was there unless you know to look for the contours in the grass. A large sunken rectangle close to the house.

Earlier it had rained. She reaches out the window and rubs her hands on the outside of the pane, pulls them back inside. She rubs her face with the grimy water, her neck, her breasts, her stomach. Nothing now but sweet dizziness.

We are at our usual posts, sitting across from each other at the kitchen table. My grandmother cuts coupons from a stack of old newspapers. She's wearing reading glasses so that the tip of her nose pokes out like a small bulb. She is tough. She still teaches a dance and exercise class for seniors, and anyone else who can keep up, on Wednesday and Friday af-ternoons at the rec center uptown. This is how I always think of her. Strong, but also tired. Not that far off from the way she looks in the old dance pictures, slinky and lovely, wrapped in a feather boa, wearing ruffled bloomers, one

beautiful foot raised above her head. Because in those pictures there's a tiredness that doesn't match her scanty-clad
showgirl poses. Her eyes look as if she's fighting to close them
—as if she already knows, as if she's a mother with a gone
daughter already.

"So Bunny never—"

"Never."

"She just denied it? The entire time?"

"More than denial. Listen, Alex, there's no mystery. That
woman would rather her daughter had been violated and
mutilated by a nutcase. She couldn't tolerate a single thing
out in the world that reflected badly on her. Especially the
truth that she was a vile mother who drove that girl to
the grave. Why else would Paula have done it like that? In
front of all those people?" My grandmother pauses, snips a
coupon. "*And* she was jealous."

"Of who?"

"Who do you think? Of me—for Esther."

"We're not talking about Aunt Esther."

"Always. We're always talking about Esther."

"But Paula—"

"Bunny Hirsh was spared."

"This was a girl who dove out a window and nobody had
any idea why. You said it yourself to Bunny on the patio."

"I watched my precious—tubes out her nose on a bed."
My grandmother rises. The scissors clatter to the table. "That
woman never even sent a card."

My Father in an Elevator with Anita Fanska, August 1976

HOT DAY. Anita Fanska. Sleeveless dress and hair wrapped up, intricately woven. Her head leaning forward looks like an attacking wicker picnic basket—and she wants him—and he most certainly wants her. Her sigh is more a moan. They've got eighteen floors to go. He says, The Fiskjohn matter, and she says, Yes, the Fiskjohn matter. My father's voice changes, gets lower. He thinks it sounds like thunder. He rumbles. The letter with the changes has to go out by tomorrow noon at the absolute latest. He hopes reminding her that he's the boss might make a difference to Anita Fanska. It doesn't, and he knows it. Authority isn't something she yields to—doesn't matter that for the past seven years she's been somebody's secretary (my father's for about a year now), and that earlier she was a Catholic schoolgirl taunting nuns. Even then people said Anita Fanska took what she wanted, which was zero from anybody, including God, as she often reminded the Sisters. She wants my father not because he's the boss and can make things simple for her, which is the reason he wants her to want him, but because he's balding and not sure of himself, and ruddy-faced, and some days he's handsome, and once he ran for the state legislature and got trounced but came into work the next day and said, breathed, *Well, that's over*—he didn't cry about it. He went back to work. She cried. Anita Fanska cried for two days; she wanted my father to be governor. She takes a step toward him, crowds him. He watches the floor numbers tick down.

Anita yanks out the stop button and sets off the alarm. She pulls off her heels and sits on her shins with her bare feet facing up behind her. As if they're on the beach and not in an elevator in the Mercantile Exchange Building on South Wacker. My father won't sit down. He stands above her, as if literally lording over her will make her stop lording over him in the only way that matters.

Mr. Burman—

The Fiskjohn matter.

Mr. Burman—

He loves her, which is his real problem, though admitting it to himself would take more than even Anita Fanska can muster right now. You come to love in so many ways—the routes zigzag and always turn into lies when you try to retrace them. It's what Anita likes best about love, the way it twists you, boggles you, and she's pretty certain it's here with this angry little man who won't sit down and join her, but who also lacks the courage to push in the button and stop the alarm. Because what he wants—submission—is so far away from what she wants, this sentimental girl who's fallen so hard for her boss. She wants to love him in this elevator amid the jangling alarm that sounds like chains being dragged, while custodians scramble and the security guards babble nonsense into their walkie-talkies.

Any people in it?

Moron, you think a rat pulled the alarm?

It's a chance at love and chances don't come around so often, and she pats the floor as if all he needs is a little coaxing.

Philip—

But my father stands on the edge of a beautiful abyss and dreams of power. He watches her sweat-glazed arms and doesn't move, does nothing, which is why the aftermath, the long office August days, will be so much easier for her—because she sat down in that elevator and simply said, Philip, and nothing else.

Seymour

SEYMOUR BURMAN dreams he's General Grant writing his memoirs while racing throat cancer. Dreams he is sitting in a wicker chair on a porch at Mount McGregor, New York, a writing board on his lap. Dreams of glorious reams of paper at his feet and of pain in his esophagus so incredible that it feels as if someone is forcing him to swallow acid, the acid like a liquid blade slicing, and yet still he writes, still he remembers, still it all comes back to him in a throb of valiant memories—until everything shoves to a halt like a marching army suddenly stopped and falling backward over itself. It's time for Shiloh. Shiloh, Shiloh. Little church called Shiloh. How do you write about Shiloh? How do you say you were in a clean-sheeted bed in Savannah, a steamship ride away from your men at Pittsburgh Landing, when the rages of hell poured forth? How do you say 41,000 rebel soldiers—who you knew were only twenty miles away—took you by surprise? How do you say you heard the thunder of the guns during your breakfast and that you finished that breakfast? Your reputation to be riddled like the uniform of another mother's son from Ohio, and still you chewed on?

Sy Burman asleep with Grant's *Personal Memoirs* riding his

chest, snoring in his chair in the den on Pine Point Drive. It's a Sunday in July 1979. The book rises and falls. My grandfather's hand aches from gripping a pen in his dreams. Grant will never use his voice to speak again. Only these paper words. Seymour, who fought his own war, loves the little bearded hog butcher hero who won the bloodiest war of all, and now he inhabits the veined, shrunken hand that will not confess the debacle of Shiloh. That will avoid it, shunt it, spend what little eloquence is left on less haunted glory. There is nothing like the oblivion that coats memories we refuse to remember. My grandfather shivers with Grant, a blanket pulled up to his chin, a wool cap on his head.

The Moraine on the Lake

THE MORAINE HOTEL. Highland Park, Illinois. The wedding was absolutely splendid. The bride radiant, unworldly. Guests could look at her for only so long. Whoever saw a dress so white? The way you might shield your eyes should you be so lucky to make it to any place like heaven. Here it was. The Moraine on the Lake. It's long gone. They knocked it down in the seventies. It was a sprawling white hotel with five sets of colonnades. To proud Midwestern eyes that had never seen one, it looked like a Southern plantation transplanted to our rocky bluffs. All that remains now are the towering oaks and the ravine that used to border the back, lakeside of the hotel, an enormous moat of dead leaves. Esther's wedding at the Moraine Hotel was splendid. Even now, that's the word people use, and it's funny that knowing what happened later can never spoil this vision of perfection. Now the pictures of it are stuffed away. But they pale. They look staged, like black-and-white movie stills. The only way to see Esther Burman's wedding is to remember it. Every once in a while the idea of it, that it happened, leaks, and people who were there are struck by the memory of her. Of course the groom was perfectly irrelevant, which makes people remember him only fondly, if they remember him at all. It was Esther. Every inch of her was glory.

* * *

Her mother, Bernice, is fussing in the hall. Esther is standing in the bedroom of the presidential suite. She is wearing a slip and waiting. Her back is to the lake that fills the window. The lake is calm, almost sullen; the waves limp and whiteless. She sees it anyway. She thinks of how even the meekest wave yanks the gravel back and forth, up the shore and back. She kisses her shoulder, not out of narcissism but out of self-preservation. She fears the splendor and the praise. The praise. She already knows to beware of it, to hate it, though her mother eats it, compliment after compliment, like her favorite Fannie May nonpareils, chocolate on one side, beady candy on the other. *Bernice, she glows. She positively glows.* At the rehearsal, one chuckler waved a half-eaten shrimp in Esther's face and gabbed: "They can see you from space. The Russians are watching you right now. You could make peace. You could melt even those cold fishes. Send Esther to fight the Reds! Send Esther!"

It could be a chant: Send Esther! Send Esther!

She kisses her shoulder to tell herself, Hold on, wait. Her mouth telling her body not to worry, that this will last only so long. That everything—she already knows this—lasts only so long.

Now she stands with her hands at her sides. Later she will wear gloves, something that will occur to her years after as the most ridiculous thing about the entire day. She won't turn around, only stares at the door and waits. It makes her woozy, the lake. She won't look at it. She will never look at it. She waits for her mother, who in a moment will bustle in and merrily gasp, "Angel, but you're not dressed!" Her hands full of a veil that will make Esther think of a heap of white lettuce.

Esther Stories

THE FACES of the pallbearers are always the same. Gallant and not trying to seem proud, but at the same time not unproud. That's the fine balance, and when we hoist, it's not our muscles but our sorrow lifting, our sorrow straining. My father lifts his sister. There are five other pairs of hands lifting, but mostly it's him, and he doesn't imagine her last moments, or any other moments before her last ones. He's concentrating on his lifting, not saying goodbye, lifting, not recriminating, lifting. He has a job to do, and he's like everybody else. His hands are no different.

I used to prance around my grandparents' house on Pine Point Drive in my Uncle Lloyd's pointy, flimsy army cap, though by that time Lloyd was already persona non grata in my family. Whenever my grandmother saw me in that hat, which I'd found in a dresser drawer in my father's old room, she'd wince and bite the inside of her cheek and say, "Take that off, Alexander. I beg you."

One theory, a romantic one, is that things started to go wrong, horribly wrong, with my Aunt Esther after she was forced to break it off with Bo, a gentile, the only man she'd ever loved. (This last nameless Bo is always described as a gentile even though his not being Jewish was never an issue: the issue was that he had no prospects and he wasn't going to college.) I'm not certain how my grandparents actually prevented my aunt from running off, but I assume (membership in this family for thirty-five years gives me at least this right) that they deployed a tried-and-true Burman tactic: psychological guerrilla warfare. Potshots from the hills under the cover of darkness. I can hear my grandmother muttering under her breath: . . . *My opinion of course doesn't mean a lick . . . only your happiness . . . never has . . . a mother's burden to suffer this . . . children do what they wish . . .* And of course in drops Lloyd Kantorowitz to the rescue! Some son of a friend of Mattie Rosenthaler's. Handsome, modest, tall, ex-lieutenant, medical student. A faintly mustached man with long eyelashes and squinting, tentative eyes, all three characteristics bothering my grandfather so much that in later years he often growled that he knew Lloyd was a smelly potato from one look at his mug.

I study an old high school picture of Esther and find it difficult to believe that the portly, angry, hollow-eyed woman who lived in my grandparents' basement throughout the 1980s is this person who looks so much like Elizabeth Taylor in *Cat on a Hot Tin Roof:* seductive, sweaty, a little nasty, a little pouty. In this black-and-white photograph in the gold frame I found tucked away in my grandfather's study, in a cabinet under his shelf of Civil War books, is someone I would have loved had I been there.

Not a surprise that at her funeral there were men like me to spare. Lonely grovelers who had known her back when.

When she was Homecoming Queen of New Trier East High School, when a single glance in your direction from Esther Burman in the slamming-locker halls was like being plucked from the masses by a long-fingered, just-widowed princess. Calling for you. Choosing you. And you pointing at your throat, confused and flushed, knowing she was making a mistake that would cut deep for years. A guy behind you or next to you, but never you. And her (the glance longer now, burning into your memory): Yes, you.

So she married Lloyd Kantorowitz in 1963, and Bo became a Burman family footnote. I first hear of all this from Olivia Hodges, my grandparents' housekeeper of forty-five years, a woman I loved as much as my mother, a woman who used to sing out family secrets as willingly as she'd serve grilled peanut butter and marshmallow sandwiches to my friends and me after school.

One day Olivia told me this: His name was Bo, but he didn't look anything like that stupid name. A short boy with crazy dirty hair. No taller than your father and very polite. Politer than your father ever was or is. From here but not from here here. (She made circles with her hand to let me know that he wasn't from near the lake, that he probably grew up on the other side of the expressway. West.) Esther said he played guitars or drums or some other nonsense. He cleaned up at your grandpapa's bank, and no way in God's emerald heaven was your nana going to let Esther end up with a man who pulled wastebaskets and swamped toilets for a living. Esther didn't take ballet and piano and those posture lessons from Cootie Thomas downtown so she could marry a janitor. Use your common sense, Alex. Esther was a jewel. I used to pin her hair every night. She wouldn't let anybody else touch it. She wouldn't even go to Lamont's with your nana. But did she eat that boy up! Talked about him night and day. Dreamed about him. Woke up in the morning, and it was Bo jumped out of a plane, Bo got elected president. Lloyd was polite, but so shy. Not like Bo, who used to come around to the kitchen window and make faces at me, wiggling his mouth trying to reach his nose with his tongue. Then out of the clear blue sky she told him not to come around the house anymore, and she went down to Illinois for college. Lloyd, when he came in the picture, would look at his shoes when he talked to me, and I'm the maid and he's the doctor. But handsome. Not a hair of a nose difference between Lloyd and Rock Hudson in the face except that Lloyd was going to be a doctor and your nana liked that better.

You can't blame Lloyd for falling in love with Esther. Who wouldn't have? Who didn't? He was from Eau Claire, Wisconsin. A Jew from some little town in Wisconsin nobody in my family could ever pronounce correctly. You think he ever saw a girl like Esther Burman before? She was a freshman at the University of Illinois and still grieving over her sent-away Bo, when my grandmother, her best friend, Mattie Rosenthaler, and Mattie Rosenthaler's friend (always unnamed, as though everyone refuses, out of principle, to remember this last link to Lloyd) conspired to introduce her to the young doctor-to-be on the Friday after Thanksgiving, 1962. Esther was a sorority girl, already treasurer of the chapter and only a first-semester freshman. (A girl dropped out and Esther leaped from pledge to officer.) Lloyd was in his third year of medical school at Northwestern. They met at a cocktail party in the house on Pine Point, in the living room. The big room with the matching black leather chairs and the long windows and the shaggy brown rug that I used to run my fingers through and pretend was the thick fur of a dead bear my grandfather shot. Petrified Lloyd made Esther laugh when he fumbled and then stepped backward on his wineglass. Together they knelt and bumped heads, Lloyd in the heat of his fifteenth apology. Then my grandmother and her friends descended upon the shards like crazy pecking pigeons. Clucking: It's not your fault, Lloyd. Olivia keeps forgetting to dry off the stems. Olivia! Help us here! It's not your fault, Lloyd!

The next Saturday Lloyd drove down to Champaign with a back seat piled high with violets and yellow roses and boxes of Fannie May chocolates. It became a regular date. Lloyd's Saturday-afternoon drive down south. After driving three and a half hours without stopping, Lloyd would sprint up to the palatial oak door, each time as jittery as the first day he met her. Then he'd be ushered inside the forbidden palace, that nation-state of women. The front hall of that sorority house was every bit as grave as any European church he'd studied in high school. Flying buttresses. Vaulted basilicas. Carpets as thick and soft as a putting green. Curtains closed tight against the street like a funeral home. The house mother, fat and stubby, an elegant noose of pearls around her neck, standing behind the little embroidered couch in the waiting room, arms folded across her tremendous chest repeating, "We have rules in this house, Mr. Kantorowitz. Hard-and-fast rules concerning curfew." Waving her chubby arms, nose crunched up as if she's whiffing something putrid. "Get acquainted with these rules lest you find yourself permanently unwelcome at Sigma Delta Tau." And then Esther would appear, a flutter of hair and unbuttoned buttons, the back of her dress floating behind her like a puffed sail, circling the couch, kissing Mrs. Roachwell, gushing, "Please don't scare Lloyd, Mother. Can't you see he's scarable?"

I shake hands with Lloyd after Esther's funeral service. He sucks his lower lip. He still has that smudge of mustache. He is still handsome. "Difficult day," he says. His hand is moist and sticky, and he holds mine too long, trying to make up for the cowardice of his words. I nod, and both of us turn away to shake more hands. Later, I watch him as he stands alone. His second wife, also a doctor, stands nearby and talks to an elderly cousin of my grandmother's, a woman in a jeweled hat named Simone. (Apparently she is French, but nobody has ever been able to explain why she's related to us.) Lloyd's new wife has heard only horror stories about Esther, but this is a funeral and she murmurs to Simone in a reverential hush. Cousin Simone yawns. She's never liked my grandmother or her children, and this whole ordeal is starting to bore her. Lloyd stands close to the edge of the conversation, but he's alone. Alone as the aged high school boys who will go home to their lipsticked wives and sigh, Rosalie, I still can't get myself to believe that Esther Burman could die. I watch Lloyd watch the spot at the front of the room where the casket lay before the men from Pritzger's loaded it into the hearse for the ride to the cemetery. Later, Lloyd and I will bump elbows as pallbearers when we help move Esther from the car to the grave. But now I watch him squint at the spot. His head quivers slightly. *If she was gone before, where is she now?*

If it is true what my grandmother says—that our boxes of family pictures lie like her cousin Ubby, the harness racetrack owner from Pittsburgh—then you should be able to tell they are frauds just by looking at them. But you can't. And who is to say, without the interference of hindsight, that Esther and Lloyd's early marriage wasn't a happy one? Esther moved back to Chicago from Champaign and into Lloyd's apartment on 1 East Schiller on the north side. Years in my family are often identified by streets: Lunt Avenue, Roger's Park. Pine Point Drive, the first house in the suburbs. In the 1 East Schiller photographs—1963 through 1965—Lloyd and Esther are attached, tangled, cheek to cheek. Their grins are smelted together to form one happy gaping mouth. (My grandfather likes to take close-ups of his subjects' faces. Backgrounds have never interested him.) To me, the smiles aren't haunting. They're beautiful, naive smiles that have no way of knowing what's to come. They make me love them. The them they were in 1963 and the them they became. Maybe it's because the pictures are only of their faces. No rooms. No houses. No familiar trees to link them to their longer story. Esther's compact little face and Lloyd's awkward tilt toward her. He was so much taller. Two smiling, bobbing apple–colored blushing cheeks.

I cannot—as my grandmother does—scoff. I refuse to see only the bitterness of later. *I should have known. We should have known. Seymour said he didn't like something he saw, but who ever took what he said for a grain of anything.* But just because I know genuine joy when I see it photographed doesn't mean I can't see, even at this early stage, what Esther's trying to do with her eyes. In every picture from that period Esther is looking straight at the camera, smiling with Lloyd but also entreating her father, my grandfather, the ubiquitous cameraman, to *see her.* I say that was the problem in those years. She let people look but not see her. Her parents, her parents' friends, her sorority sisters, her husband. Except for those moments—caught on film and now stored in a box in the basement—when she can be seen begging her father to put the camera down and look at her and just say, *Esther.*

Not a letter opener she attacked him with but a butter knife —a blunt, rounded, harmless knife for slicing butter is what my grandmother says. Olivia insists it was a letter opener. Take your pick. What matters is Esther chasing Lloyd around the apartment screaming and finally cornering him in the shower stall. Pushing, digging the blade—whichever blade— into his shoulder as he crouched. Ripping his shirt and then his flesh. Lloyd not fighting her because he never, even then, refused her touch.

Oh! I tell you! Olivia shouted. Nothing was bigger in that house than when Esther was expecting and the celebrating was going on. Mattie Rosenthaler, and all your nana's other friends, too, brought over enormous boxes of presents from Field's, and your nana couldn't stop rubbing her hands. What could be better to cure what people called Esther's restlessness than a baby? Everybody shopped and shopped, and Esther glowed like a little pink peach, like she did in high school when she won Homecoming Queen and rode the float through town. All of us smiling in front of your grandpapa's bank, and we waved and she waved. When she was pregnant she'd take the train out from the city and rub her belly, and I remember her saying, Ollie, do you believe it? Can you be- lieve I'm the swelly-belly girl! And I cried and said, Esther, I love you, honey. You've got to take care of yourself now. Because even then, even though that girl was happier than she ever was, she was starting to doubt things. She'd say things like Lloyd doesn't love me and he never has. Course I knew that wasn't the problem ever. Oh, did I know that wasn't it! Lloyd loved her like you've never seen. She didn't want to be her. Makes no sense in a girl so beautiful, but it's true. So beautiful that people used to stop the carriage when she was a baby. We'd be walking along and people would shout and point and say, Would you look at that angel. An angel on earth. But when she got older Esther used to stand in front of the mirror and stare and stare at herself as if she could change what she'd been given just by looking.

My parents were out of town, so we were sleeping at my grandparents'. I must have been eight or nine, my brother around four. It was late and I was tippytoeing across the cold tile of the big kitchen on my way to Olivia's room, and the cats. I liked to sleep with Olivia, my face in a soft cat belly, my feet rubbing Olivia's tough bony ankles. I had almost made it to Olivia's door when someone sniffed. I turned and looked. It was Esther. It must have been sometime in 1968, because she had no stomach anymore. When I tried to sneak by, she stopped me. I looked at her again and, in the weak light of the driveway lamp, saw that she was wearing only a towel.

"Alex?"

"Uh-huh."

She was eating cold spaghetti. She put her fork in the bowl. "I want to tell you something your mother's not going to tell you."

"Okay."

"And I want you not to forget."

"I won't."

"You're going to sleep with Olivia?"

"Just to say hi to the cats."

"If I tell you something, will you remember it?"

"Okay."

Even in that low light I could see that her eyes were red and she was more beautiful than my mother.

"I'm going to be honest with you."

"Okay."

"You pay." She stared at me. "You pay for everything. When you think you're getting something for free—remember this—you'll pay for it later." She put her bowl down on the counter and came closer, knelt down. Her breath was hot. The driveway light was in her hair. "Please don't forget this, and don't let anybody, especially a pretty Miss Muffet, tell you I lied to you." Then she held my arms for about a minute before she laughed a little and said, "You can laugh in this house. Even when Olivia's not around to make jokes. You are allowed to laugh."

My younger brother, Joey, remembers little about Esther. But he thought about it for a while and then said, "I spent one day with her in my entire life. I must have been six or something. Mom brought us downtown because you had to go to the doctor's or the barber. For some reason she dropped me off at Esther's apartment. Uncle Lloyd wasn't home. It was a Saturday. She took me to the Shedd Aquarium to see the electric eels. Then we went to a park. Grant probably. She chased me around. We played horses. She got down on her knees and neighed. She let me climb a tree also. I remember that. And she didn't tell me to be careful. She just let me climb. Then she took me to Granny Goodfox on Wells Street and bought me a felt puppet, a cow. In the car on the way home, Mom named it 'Bossy.' I remember you kept swinging it around by its ear out the window until Mom told you to cut it out."

Her baby was born dead on February 10, 1968. They named her Frances after some great-grandmother of Lloyd's and buried her at the Burman plot in Memorial Park in Skokie. For the first six months after it happened, my grandmother often slept on a cot at Esther and Lloyd's apartment. Either that or Esther stayed at Pine Point. My grandmother told me many years later that at first Lloyd resisted, but later tolerated her presence, because at least when she was around Esther stopped her terrible moaning. In that same conversation I asked, Did Esther really want to be a mother? I mean, given everything you know now, do you think she would have been able to handle it? We were sitting at her kitchen table. This was last year. My grandmother glared, but not at me, somewhere off to her left, as if somebody else, not me, had spoken. Then she said, "What kind of question is that? Don't get so big, Mr. Toots, that you stop being able to understand that that baby would have rescued everybody."

The house on Pine Point Drive was a dirty-yellow-bricked rectangular colonial covered by scraggly vines, as though the house was trying to camouflage itself behind the trees in the front yard. In the back yard was an old swing set, rusted out, one swing cracked in half, the other missing, its two chains dangling. There was also an old wooden boat—even then overgrown by weeds—that was the one thing my grandfather brought north from the old house on Lunt Avenue. The boat was our favorite, and I'd always race my brother to it. We'd start at the garage, run through the garden (with Olivia shouting about her cabbages), and if Joey didn't trip me, I'd win.

True, her beauty made it easier for everybody, because nobody really had to look at her. It created the distance that nobody even knew existed until much later. But in my family there was also a little boy who grew up to be my father. While everyone else may have loved Esther's beauty without looking into her eyes, my father saw someone else. The Esther she wanted my grandfather to see from behind his camera. And he hated her. Olivia says it's because he thought his head was too round and he was too short and because he was older and because nobody ever repeated his name, called him angel, nothing. My father saw only the flawed, scared, restless Esther. The tantrum Esther. The Esther who used to go into fits as late as her sixteenth birthday. Ranting on the kitchen floor, screaming about her hair, and throwing her shoes at Olivia.

What it was between them I'll never know. I have two brothers, two sisters myself. One of my brothers must have been the dumbest hoodlum in Chicago for five, ten years running. Little Davey Jr. We all called him Dodge. I didn't speak to him the last year of his life. I might see him again, depending, and if I do, you can bet I'll call him a horse's ass to his face, even as I'm kissing it. But Esther and your dad had something else. Like they weren't ever related. He was, what? Four years older? Since she was little he used to go after her. When your papa was away at the war, it was just your nana, me, and the kids. Your nana loved that girl so much, sometimes she forgot she had a son. Your dad used to follow me around. Yanking my dress. And when he wasn't pulling on me, he was tugging Esther's hair like he was plucking weeds, and calling her a liar about everything. That never stopped. Even after she got married—even after he found your mom and was married himself—he still said Esther was a selfish fool. Then he went after Lloyd. Both your papa and your dad thought Lloyd wasn't good enough for this family because he couldn't talk as fast as they could. The more your nana went on about his face his nose his cheeks, his being a doctor, the more those two complained about him. But who they were really talking about was Esther.

This one always gets told with a grin, no matter who the teller. How one night Lloyd drove Esther eighteen miles out of Champaign, to a little town called Rantoul. The Rantoul story. How they cuddled up on a mowed-down cornfield with a bottle of wine and a blanket to see how many stars they could count. Lloyd kept a tally on a dollar. But Lloyd forgot to fill up the car after his drive downstate and they ran out of gas coming home at 10:45. Curfew was 11:00. They walked the eight miles back. Mrs. Roachwell standing at the door at half past midnight. Howling: Banned. Banned! Banned for life, Lloyd Kantorowitz!

After the service my grandmother weeps softly into her palm in the front row, grabbing and reeling in with her free hand anyone fearless enough to go near her murmuring grief, her shivering.

* * *

My father says now, even now, that he helped put her in the paddy wagon that brought her to the locked psychiatric unit at Rush St. Luke's out of family duty and love. They brought a white-and-blue-striped Chicago police paddy wagon, and my father, in lieu of her nowhere-to-be-found, soon-to-be-ex husband, helped put her in it out of family duty, out of love, he says. He rips open a sugar packet with his teeth. I know you'd never believe that I did it out of kindness, and I did not. Out of love, because she was my sister and nobody else gave a damn. That worthless Lloyd. You think he cared for a minute what happened to her? After she attacked him with the scissors he knew he had a way out. And then, when he finally did leave, all that screeching and pounding Esther started doing on the apartment walls.

Nana says it was a butter knife.

Listening to my mother. No wonder.

And Olivia said the neighbor's baby was bothering her, that it kept crying in its sleep.

A baby, bless Olivia's heart! An old faggot lived next door, Alex! I knew him, a judge, lived into his nineties still chasing young clerks around his chambers. There wasn't a baby for miles of that apartment. Don't you get it? What choice did I have? Let her keep at it? You think I wanted to admit—even to myself—that we had a lunatic in the family? Your grandmother wanted nothing more than to let it all go on. She said that neighbor probably *was* bothering her. She said, What could Esther do but bang on the walls if management wouldn't listen to her? *Don't you see what I'm up against with these people?* But your mother has trained you so well to see me as the enemy in every situation that you can't, won't—so easy to judge me now. What could be easier than to judge me now?

Your sister.

My sister, yes.

Lloyd and that dirty little mustache, my grandmother says.
Running off with a nurse. Mortifying is what it was. Facts
have never been very important to her. Lloyd ran off with another doctor. But wasn't the leap into another set of warm
arms inevitable, a survival instinct? Doesn't matter to anybody except my grandmother what job she had. *A nurse, a
little nurse, how obvious.* If it makes her rest easier, let her be a
nurse. The point is that Lloyd's leaving gave my grandmother
somewhere to put the blame. For all of it. The divorce and
the hospitalization. For her, the two went hand in hand.

"Oh, for God's sake, the man is an adulterer!" my grandmother roared into the phone one afternoon. I must have
been fourteen. Olivia and I were watching baseball. She said
of course Nana was talking to Mattie Rosenthaler. "A tiff. Little more than a tiff," Nana was saying. "A husband and wife
do that a thousand times a day in this state. And that's
grounds? While he runs off with the Red Cross, the court
says her nicking him is grounds?" Olivia shaking her head
and clapping for the do-nothing Cubs.

Olivia's hair has always been white (even in the oldest pictures). The story about her that got whispered is that once
she ran away from the family to marry a man. She went to
Gary, Indiana, because her husband worked in the steel mills.
This was after my father was born but before Esther. She
came back after exactly a year. My grandmother said she
never said a word about the man, not even his name, but my
brother and I used to make up stories about him. We called

him Gary from Gary, and said he had arms as long as the antennas on the top of the John Hancock Building.

The week after Olivia came back from being married, Dr. Zaballow slapped my grandmother on the behind and told her she was pregnant again.

Always white except when she wore one of her black wigs, which she did when she bartended my grandmother's cocktail parties. I can see her laughing at Lloyd and his slippery fingers and even dumber feet. Thanksgiving, 1962. Stooping to clean up the glass and then pouring him another wine. Patting his round shoulders and saying, Doctor, can't you prescribe something for my aching back? Forty-eight years old and already my aching back. Lloyd gulping and coughing: I'm certainly not a physician yet.

Watching, jealous already, my father stands in the corner of the room near the bar and talks to one of my grandfather's friends about his future plans. He's finally finished college, but is still adrift. He seethes over Lloyd because Lloyd is tall and, though a klutz, is already someone.

She tried to kill him.

She didn't try to kill him. Even you can't say that with a straight face.

She stabbed him. There was blood. Doesn't matter whether she used a Bic pen or a machete. The standard for involuntary civil commitment is dangerousness. Do you want me to fax you a copy of the statute?

But they didn't take her away until six months later. Up till then Lloyd was still living there. He lived there *after*, Dad. If he was so scared—

She was in hysterics. Even the old judge called my office

and pleaded that I do something. Her attacking his walls all night. The man said it sounded like a riot next door. And Lloyd barely lived there after. In name alone. Since when are you so technical? She never denied attacking him. Anyway, you're missing the whole point. She stopped eating, wouldn't answer the phone. The woman needed help. Why do you refuse to see that? I'm to blame for what went on in that apartment? The same as your grandmother. You never look to the source. Take a look at Esther. Take a look at her life. Take a look at what she cared about from the day she was born.

"You can't get all crazy over the little things now that you're toting a baby," Olivia told her. "Because then the baby'll be born with nerves like yours and then we'll all be in for it." And Esther laughed and said, "Ollie, don't talk that way. The kid'll hear you. He's got ears in his feet."

In a box in the basement of my grandparents' new house, the flat ranchhouse we haven't even bothered to christen with the name of its address, I root out another picture. This one of my father in a sailor suit. Esther in a red dress between his knees. My grandfather has taken a few steps back (the kids probably waved him away), so it's one of those rare photographs where there is a background. You can see the sides and the pointy bow of the rowboat. The trees in the yard of the Lunt Avenue house. They're sitting in the stern; my father holds his hand like a little roof over his eyes, as though captaining the boat through violent sun. His other hand is clasped around his sister's waist. You can see the tips of his fingers. Esther's eyes are closed, but her cheeks are raised in delight.

* * *

The bike accident story gets tossed around. I first heard it from my mother, who wasn't born a Burman (and like Lloyd had the sense to get out) but knows much of the lore, because a long time ago—no longer, God knows, no longer, she says —she was intrigued by the family antics. So she asked questions. She said that the way she understood it, Esther fell off her bicycle when she was eleven. She hit a crack in the sidewalk in front of the house on Pine Point, flipped forward over the handlebars, and landed on her head. Spent a week and a half in the hospital with multiple concussions. Her face was pretty mangled. If you look closely at some of the old pictures, you can see a scar that begins over her left eye and disappears into her hair. And though the doctors said she was a hundred percent golden, it has always been my grandmother's private belief (this from Olivia, not my mother) that Esther never fully recovered from falling off her bike.

I have this not-so-distant memory. A day on my father's sailboat on Lake Michigan in 1984, four years before Esther's death. She is there with us. She wears dark sunglasses. My brother and my grandparents are there, too. An afternoon of sailing, an attempt at reconciliation years after Lloyd's flight, the time at Reed Hospital, Esther's move home. The day had been uneventful. My father made a point of staying away from the cockpit, away from Esther, and spent most of the afternoon fiddling with the sails, winching and rerigging. My grandmother and Esther mostly stared at the lake and sometimes spoke about the proper amount of suntan lotion and whether the buildings in the distance were Waukegan or Lake Forest. It happened, as a lot of things do in this family, just when we were about to leave each other.

My brother and I have already helped our grandparents

into the dinghy, the small motorboat which will take us from our mooring, in the middle of the harbor, back to the dock. My father offers Esther his hand. She waves him off—saying she doesn't need any help. Then her foot tangles in the lifeline and she trips, falls into the boat, lands in the dinghy kid's lap. My father does not laugh, only says, "Jesus, Esther, I told you and now look, you killed the kid."

"Fuck off, Philip," Esther says mildly.

My father steps down into the boat and sits next to me. We sway. He faces Esther. He says, "I work my ass off, taking you out here. Buy you lunch. The whole time you sit—and now you talk to me like dirt. You think I'm dirt?" Esther stares at him. Then she opens her little yellow purse and takes her wallet out. Yanks a twenty-dollar bill, balls it, and throws it at my father. We're puttering along in the boat now, all six of us squeezed, knees mashed together. The ride lasts no more than forty seconds, from my father's boat to the dock. My father flings the money back at her. Esther picks it up from the dirty puddle of brown water between them. They are both in their forties. I am twenty-three and home from college and hot and sweaty and want off this little boat. My grandmother wears a white headband and a plastic visor. My grandfather dons his navy cap. My grandmother yawns loudly. My grandfather feels his breast pockets for cigarettes. Though I cannot see my brother's eyes—he is sitting behind me—I know he is reading for the thousandth time the names that are printed in wavy letters on the sterns of boats bigger than my father's. *Unfazed, Wilmette, Illinois. Part-time Lover, Chicago, Illinois.* Again, my aunt throws the soggy money back. It lands in my father's lap. He picks it up again, crumples it. This time it hits Esther's shoulder and she leaves it.

Now she stares over the boat at the oily water slushing into small white waves. I don't look at my father, whose face is splotched red, watching the money. I grab the bill and stuff it in my pants, and half-mutter at the dinghy kid, who looks about twelve: "In this family you pick up the crumbs." But the kid doesn't laugh, knows this isn't funny. He knows it should be, but there's something about these people that makes it not funny. This ignoring older woman in white and the daydreaming captain. These two graying, infantile throwers, brother and sister. When Esther noticed the money was gone, she looked at me and said, "Split it with your brother."

Oh, those people couldn't tell you you have a cold. But they shuttled her around for tests. And then more tests. Tests tests. You wouldn't believe how many hospitals there are in Chicago where you can get a test. Enormous hospitals ten blocks long you never even heard of. Finally, Reed Mental Heath Center. Out near Palos Heights, wherever that is. They gave her a nice room. It had wallpaper, cream-colored. They tried to make it homey, and I give them credit for that. Say what you want about those people, and of course they're all monsters, but that's what they get paid for. Her diagnosis changed every week. The liars. But even so, they treated her well, and Esther . . . You know how Esther is in any social situation, even after all that. She organized things. A drama club. Gave piano lessons. She led nature walks. A troop of foot-dragging loons following Esther by a couple of feeble trees, and Esther would say, That's a dutch elm, that's a white birch. She didn't know any more about trees than I do. Certainly no one wanted it to happen. And your father? No. I'm going to leave him out of this—he did what he thought was right, and there was no arguing with him. But once it happened, I was against it. Understand that. Remember it. I went to the court and screamed at the judge, and they had to practically carry me out. One of the police officers whispered that if I wasn't careful I'd follow my daughter to the bin. Times were different then—if he said that now I'd write a letter to the governor and get him fired. But finally it was better for her. I'll say that. The drugs, yes. But also the stability. At Reed she didn't have to carry herself. Go to the store. Visiting her made the whole thing look tempting, let me tell you . . . And she didn't hate me as much when she lived there. Of course you know that changed, and she let me know the devil she thought I was. Don't care about anybody too much, Alex. You aren't doing them any favors.

"I don't feel the kicking anymore."

"You're just getting nervous because it's close to the time."

"Lloyd."

"It's not unusual for the movement to lessen toward term. Many studies have shown—"

"No shifting. Nothing. A week ago it was kicking and now—"

"It's normal. Don't get upset. I'm telling you."

"No. I don't feel any kicking."

Because he refused to stop loving her. Not because she was jealous. Not about who he was screwing in the linen closets at the hospital. I watch Lloyd watch the spot at Pritzger's where they took Esther's casket away. With all the people who knew her chatting quietly, respectfully . . . After the baby died. Because he assaulted her with his optimism and his willful infuriating blindness. This I don't need anyone to tell me across the kitchen table over coffee. That screaming, that jabbing. Because Lloyd couldn't see that the death of her baby was punishment for giving in so easily.

It's what he could never understand. He thought she'd settle into her life because that's what people did. He bumps shoulders with his new pretty doctor wife, but doesn't feel her. He hears his wife conversing with the little French woman. Their words mean nothing. Twelve years since he last saw Esther, but the wall that time built has always been hollow.

They released her after ten months. (My grandmother had been telling anyone outside her closest circle that Esther was traveling abroad.) The divorce decree gave her next to nothing because of the evidence of physical abuse. She had nowhere else to go, so my grandparents gave her Olivia's old basement room, the room Olivia had slept in during the four years she lived in the new house before she retired and moved home to the city to live with her sister full time. My grandfather got Esther a job at a credit bureau in Wheeling—she'd always been strong with numbers. At my grandfather's urging she'd been an accounting major at Illinois (although she never got a degree). Everyone was grateful that numbers seemed to come back quickly for her. After six months at home, she even bought a car. She was thirty-nine when she moved back in with my grandparents. She told my grandmother she was going to move out soon, but she never did. By all accounts she got along well at work. Her employer—a thick-necked man who kept honking into a napkin—spoke lovingly of her at the funeral: *She was the one everyone in the office went to. You see? Esther understood things, outside-of-work things.* She made a few friends and used to go out for drinks with them at the Wooden Nickel in Highwood. At home, she was silent most of the time. While my grandparents no longer hosted parties, they often went to them. On some weeknights Esther ate dinner with my grandparents, but most nights she ate alone downstairs. Soups out of a cup heated in the microwave. Simple salads. Noodles. She never appeared on holidays. After the money toss on the boat she refused outright to go to my father's house, and would not come up from the basement if he was present, so I rarely saw her during those years. I do know that she read considerably during the last eight years of her life. I often noticed gaps on my grandfather's shelf of Harvard Classics. Writers like Hugo and Dostoevsky were often missing, but also the other names —the ones I'd never heard of—were gone too: *Valera, Björnson, Daudet, Kielland, Musset.*

I remember she came into my grandfather's study once while my brother and I were over. My father wasn't around. She sat silent. I watched her scan my grandfather's bookshelf as we sat and talked, and my grandfather laughed, leaned back in his swivel chair and told us his own most famous story. I was too old for the war, you understand? But that wasn't going to stop me, no sir. Signed up for the local Coast Guard out of a sense of duty, a man has to have a sense of duty. And so they sent me out to search for Hitler's submarines in the Calumet River on the southwest side! This was the part of the story when, on cue, my brother and I had always laughed when we were younger. We did that day, too. My grandfather pointed at us and shouted: But no, boys! I didn't laugh! I went—patriot that I was and am—and scoured every inch of that river for sauerkraut. Ha! Did such a good job they sent me to the South Pacific. I watched her not listening, never listening—how many times had she heard all this?—looking over the books. She was plumper and shorter, it seemed, almost squat, but her face was still the face of Esther Burman from the high school photographs. The high-arched eyebrows, small mouth, tightly pulled-back hair. She was wearing new white running shoes. Suddenly she stood. She waited until we all stopped talking and looked at her. Then she left the room without a wave or a nod.

And some weeknights during those years, my grandfather would shut himself in his study with his Scotch and the *Tonight Show* and Esther would blame my grandmother for everything. Slam the microwave door and say, Look what you created. And my grandmother would sit at the glass table in the kitchen (out the window, in the dark, my grandfather's little tomato garden) and whisper, I only wanted the best for you. Only the best, but even your father (and what does he ever notice?) knew that Lloyd was a nothing and I should have known, too. *It's not Lloyd, Mother. It's never been Lloyd. What's it going to take for you to understand?* But running off with a nurse like that. It's enough to make you retch. *That you insisted. It's not what you insisted on that ruined me.* I never forced. You make it sound like I had a gun to your head. *I didn't say force. Christ, if you forced I might have known better than to listen to any of it. Any of it!* And then, this is what my grandmother told me, Esther would know that was wrong, that they were both wrong about everything, and she would start to shriek. Then the shriek would turn into a gagging laugh that sounded like choking, and my grandfather would stand and turn up the volume on Johnny Carson.

Esther's grave lies next to her daughter's. The gray markers are flush to the grass, modest, but solid. The man in the cemetery office tells me that they are made of pressure-tested granite from Barre, Vermont. "It's a perpetual stone," he says.

With my index finger I smooth away the dirt from the valleys in letters.

Beloved Daughter and Mother

And yes I want to say something. I hadn't known that I would, but I do now. That one way of looking at you, and what I know of you is that so much of your life was a begging off and a begging off until—that was the cruelty. That when you finally dared, you lost.

"So Esther knew before it happened?"

"Not for certain. How could she have known for certain? I suppose she couldn't have. But yes, a month before, she called me—not crying—and said, 'Mother, Lloyd says everything is fine, that they often stop moving, but I know. A mother knows.' She was right."

Esther Burman died of breast cancer on October 27, 1988. It was fast and deadly, and my grandmother drove her to the hospital every other day for treatment and finally, to stay for good, and Esther screamed and swore at her because she didn't want to die in spite of what most people thought. A cruelty of the cancer was that she was so drugged she couldn't read novels. My grandmother sat in the silence as her daughter stared at the turned-off television. Another hospital, this one a normal one—one she could tell people at the club about—but so much worse.

Like my father, I never went to see her in that last hospital, either.

* * *

I stand in front of Olivia and her sister's house on West Van Buren. Late October 1989. Most of the leaves have fallen to the little brown lawn in front of the house, a low bungalow squeezed between two squat brick apartment buildings. A couple of boys on bicycles chase each other down the street. Olivia shouts from the screen door. Her sister Mag hovers behind her with a plate heaped with brownies and cookies and chocolates. I hug Olivia hard; she is still strong and feels— like she always did—pillowy and starchy. Her white hair pulled back tight and there is far less of it. A hollowing, some sinking below her eyes, makes me want nothing more than to curl up with her and just lie there. She's laughing. Her sister's laughing. Aleeeeeeeeeeex. Aleeeeeeeeeeex. Olivia yanks me into the house and pushes me into a puffy chair and sits down so close our knees and feet touch. The living room is crowded with chairs; the coffee table has been taken over by framed photographs. So many relatives, aunts, uncles, cousins, and I never knew a single one. The blinds are half drawn. Thin lines of dusty afternoon light crisscross the room.

"Esther's dead," I say.

"You think I was born last Tuesday? I know Esther's dead. A year ago this month she passed."

"Nana didn't want to upset you."

"Upset herself! The business of that! I raised the girl. Upset me!"

"Nana was so devastated. She couldn't even think—"

"You're telling me about it? Now she calls me twice a week to cry about it. But don't think I didn't give her a taste of lip for not telling me about the funeral. What do you want to protect an old woman from? What haven't I seen already?

You'd think nobody ever died on me, with that woman calling me with news that's not news anymore."

"That poor girl's life," Mag says. "Ravaged."

"Nana couldn't even walk into the funeral home," I say. "We had to hold her up. You know what it would take for her to accept help like that."

Olivia nods slowly and laughs a little. "Sometimes she went around like she never had a housekeeper her whole life. That woman. I can see her. Grieving enough for everybody."

"She calls to talk about Esther?"

"Yes, twice a week. Some days I put the phone down on the counter and just let her go on. My ears get tired. I do the crossword. Ask Mag. Sometimes three times a week."

"It's true," Mag says.

"But enough of that. Enough." Olivia whaps my knee. "Talk about you."

Mag brings tea. She's a large woman with a soft step across the carpet; she loves to have guests. Not to talk to them, but to serve them, watch them, anticipate them. Olivia used to talk to her on the kitchen phone for hours while Mag uh-huhed. I know, because I used to listen from my grandfather's study. And if I was hungry I'd pick up the phone—then hang it up right away, pick it up, hang it up, pick it up. I did it till Olivia started hollering across the house that if I dared do that one more time she'd call her lawyer on me. Her lawyer, my father.

"You look like you did when I was twelve."

"Don't lie to this face, Alex. I'm so old. I never thought people got so old."

"You don't look so old."

"Old as your grandpapa. Born in the same month. August 1909."

"He's back to fighting the Japanese full-time."

"Well, that man. That's what he was about. That war. Only thing that didn't bore Mr. Burman was that over-with war."

"Esther," I say, "do you mind—"

"Uh-oh, Mag. Here he goes. Don't I always say this one's the poker. Always meddling in boxes. Sniffing around in the backs of drawers, my purse. Always eavesdropping people. Used to drive his grandmother to howling for the police. Alex at her bedroom door listening to her on the phone, with his ear pressed up against the bottom of one of her good cocktail glasses."

"When Esther was pregnant—"

"What kind of boy listens to two old gossips talking about nonsense?"

"There's something I think I remember. I just want to know if—"

"Oh, Alex, please. Leave her be. You waste time."

Olivia turns to her sister. "She used to call herself the swelly-belly girl. Used to take the train out to us and walk around rubbing her stomach like a basketball."

"I remember you telling me," Mag says, handing me the plate again.

With my free hand I tug Olivia's arm. "The time when I found that cat. Wasn't Esther in the house that day?"

"That kitty!" Olivia grabs hold of Mag, who has tried to escape to the kitchen for more of everything. "Listen, honey. We had three cats already and Mr. Burman hated every single one of them. He'd howl about wringing their necks every time one of them brushed his ankle. And this one goes outside and hauls in another one."

"It was just sitting there under the swings."

"Most adorable thing you ever saw. One gray paw. Well, the other cats are already starting to hiss, so I put the kitty in Mrs. Burman's downstairs powder room, with a heap of dirt."

"For litter," Mag says. "I think I heard this story. And then the Grandpa comes home early from the bank."

"And he had to go to the bathroom," I said. "Came in, didn't say hello, marched straight to the bathroom."

Olivia laughs. "Yeah, but we didn't know that yet. That man was always barging by people with his head down like that. Man moved through houses like Dick Butkus. That day was no different. How could I know he was going to use Mrs. Burman's powder room? He never set foot in there. Room was smaller than he was. But something made him, and he opens the door and starts hollering about the pile of dirt like he never saw dirt before. Then he saw kitty hiding behind the toilet and yelled, 'Ollie—there's a goddamn skunk in the bathroom.'"

"Right. He went a little berserk."

"And then—"

"Esther. You remember?"

She turns to me and her eyes aren't laughing anymore. "Alex—"

"But she was there?"

"Yes. I remember. She shouted at everybody to come into the living room. She said, Forget about your cats, folks. Forget the skunks, everyone . . ."

I nod.

"You got it," Olivia says, because she knows I hear it, too. "That girl saying, 'This baby's dancing, dancing up a storm.' And she stood up on the couch and let us feel her, and maybe it was true, but I didn't feel anything. 'Dancing the cha-cha,' she said. And your papa standing by the door in his tie. He even smiled. 'The cha-cha, my ass,' he says."

"The turkey trot," Mag says, and guffaws. "That's some nuthouse over there."

"She said cha-cha?" I ask.

"Like it was this morning," Olivia says.

We sit for a while, the three of us, looking at the carpet, at the pictures on the coffee table. Boys in school photographs against powder blue backgrounds, canned smiles. Then Olivia whispers like Mag's in the kitchen and can't hear us, as if this is something not for Mag's ears, even though she's sitting right there with us. *All she wanted was to kiss that baby alive.* And I look at Mag, who's staring at one of the pictures as if all this reminds her of someone else.

The scuttling together people do by a window during a storm. We are like that. The funeral will be closed casket. This is the private family viewing. My father steps closer and looks at her. Esther's hands are twined so tight they make a single fist. Then he removes a hand and touches her. This sister in beige taffeta, heavy makeup, a wig. He does this. It's a part of your story even if you don't want it. He takes his hand out of his pocket and reaches into the casket, and at least one finger touches your fist. Skin that never met in life. My grandmother presses her wet forehead into the back of my neck and murmurs.

Knuckles meet the sorority house door, but softly. Though he's been running, he doesn't want to knock yet. The door hard and looming beneath his fingers. It's this moment he wants. The almost seeing her, not the seeing. Years later, after the first of many ends, Lloyd will still conjure this beautiful almost. His hesitant approach down the long corridor toward their apartment, his fear, his shoes noiseless across the carpet. The unlocking of their door. Her emergence from the bedroom that was never his even when it was his to sleep in. How it all whirls him back. *Mrs. Roachwell, Mrs. Roachwell, I'm coming. Tell that boy to stop shaking in his boots!* That first burst of Esther into any room.

The Waters

T HEY DIDN'T HAVE a dime. Nobody they knew did either (except their daughter's husband, Seymour, and he probably stole it); it was 1939. But when Rachel Shlansky wanted something, it was only a question of when. So they gave their store away for a song—"Ten Cents a Dance," Louie crooned—and moved south to Hot Springs, Arkansas, where they opened a small café on East Malvern, around the corner and three blocks down from Bathhouse Row. Rachel waited on the tables. Louie cooked behind a screen so people couldn't see his shakes.

Louie Shlansky was a gaunt, kind, terribly short-legged man with an acid tongue and no bite, who loved to tell stories on himself. They were all lies, worse than lies. Rachel called them perversions, but Louie loved to make people laugh; he didn't give a damn how. Besides, his philosophy was that stories are more believable when yours truly is the punch line. Rachel, who was literal about everything, used to tell people, No, I was there the whole time, and nothing even remotely like that happened. But after the shakes attacked him, a little man, with such vengeance, she let him have whatever joys were left. It didn't take much for her to hold her tongue while

he blathered onward. Like his famous and always-more-stu-
pid-than-the-last-time-he-told-it nonsense about the time
the police mistook him for a ranking member of the Chicago
branch of the Purple Boys. You want to know? I'll tell you.
You ever been to Bedlam? Two cops, Cheesus, running me
down like I'm Jew Kid Grabiner. Look at me. I look anything
like Jew Kid Grabiner to you? So I'm hightailing two miles,
no seven, seven miles, before I fall down a manhole on South
Halsted. The dumb paddies tumble in behind me, so the
three of us are down there groping in the dark, and one of
them goes, Anybody got a light? And I say, You kidding? I've
got cigars! And the other cop says, See, I knew this guy was a
Purple Boy, and they start whacking me with their sticks, and
I'm shouting, Boys, boys, you got it all wrong, I'm a butter-
and-egg man, I only do sundries on the side!

Behind his back and sometimes in front of it, his pals in
Roger's Park called Rachel "the claw." To them she was a
fiend, a woman with moles on both cheeks the size of cow's
nipples. She was the local eyesore. But she was also, as everybody well knew, the brains (and the brawn) behind their operation. Louie was owner of Louie's in name only. It was her
place, and she'd lorded over it for more than twenty-five years
from her post at the cash register. Then one day something
happened, her brain clogged up, and she dragged Louie away,
away to die in Arkansas. More bizarre is that she did it in
the middle of some of the blackest days anybody'd ever seen.
But Rachel, hard as she was, used to wail in her sleep after
seeing him in such pain. She read in a pamphlet that the
warmer climate and yes, the waters, the miracle thermal
baths of Hot Springs, could ease some of the worst of symp-
toms, the ceaseless trembling, for one. She was a hard woman

and maybe hideous to look at, his friends said, but she loved that man without embarrassment, which was more than they could say for their own wives. And though she spent much of their mutual working day berating him for his generosity (whenever she was in the back room, Louie smuggled groceries to people without writing it on a tab), everybody knew she babied him behind the closed doors of their apartment upstairs. She washed him; Louie Shlansky never slept on sheets that weren't crisp. Rachel decreed it. Hot Springs. And they were going to open that café they talked about when they were first married, those days when their bodies were still young and unravaged. At first he protested: What about Bernice and the babies? And our customers? This block will starve. Is that what you want? To start another potato famine? This is how it started in Ireland. The best people left and then came the fungus.

She knew losing his audience alone might kill him. But what's the use of an audience when all you've got is soil in your throat? "Imagine the shaking stopping," she whispered fiercely. "Imagine it." She stroked his cheek with the inside of her fist. They were in the kitchen. In the gloom of early morning in chill Chicago April. Outside, it looked the gloom of December. It was Sunday and the store would be shut all day in deference to the law, but they'd long made a habit of getting up at 5:45 every morning. He looked at her and didn't exactly agree; surrendered would be a better word, since it wasn't, finally, up to him. If she hadn't shooed him away so she could swamp the floor, he would have told her he was grateful. He so rarely thought of himself, the self he didn't invent. Strange to think that his comfort was so important you had to pick up and move a house.

In the kitchen that morning, he didn't need to tell her he was grateful. She knew. In the ash light, she knew. She also knew that whatever she did, his was a fragile life; the move alone might kill him. But she would never be able to forgive herself for standing pat. Hot Springs. Lucky Luciano and Al Capone went there. Jack Dempsey. George Raft. Eleanor Roosevelt, too. The Illinois Central and the Chicago and Rock Island took the rich down there in sleeping cars. They came from the East Coast and Hollywood to promenade the clean white sidewalks and bathe. Rachel's pamphlet said that at Hot Springs you were either about to take your bath, taking your bath, or just getting through with your bath. There were stories of cripples walking again, even running, climbing trees, after a day or two in those waters.

One week before they left, she gave a party in his honor. All of the 800 block of Fargo Avenue crowded into the flat above the store. Louie stood, as usual, inside the circle, his wine sloshing, telling about the time his secondhand zeppelin crashed into the Indian Ocean and he got rescued by a canoe-load of Potawatomi squaws who thought he was handsome and so scalped him for free even though their normal price was $3.50. "It's why I have no hair," he said. Rachel stayed in the kitchen, silent.

Her frivolous daughter, Bernice, the dancer, whirls in, balancing two glasses in each palm. Just had another baby, a daughter, Esther, and now look at her. Already slim and careless. Overdressed as usual tonight. Pearls in a year like this. Can you imagine? Bernice sets the plate and the glasses safely on the table, widens her eyes and implores, again, "This is madness. Look how happy—"

"What! I die for that man every day and you come here all tarty and—"

"Nobody else can love him?"

"How much did you pay for those pearls?"

"Hot Springs, Mother. You'll make him a servant. The kind of money people throw around down there, you don't understand."

"I asked you never to speak of money in this house."

"I can't have an opinion. Only you can—"

"You bring shame."

"Traipsing him off to a place he doesn't know a soul? Him? Who loves nothing more than sitting on the stoop with Manny and Uncle Nort."

"You don't know."

"How do you expect him to cook in some restaurant if he can no longer even work the stock in the store? Anyway, Seymour says he can find a place for him. That he can sit at a desk. He wanted me to tell you."

Rachel's face twitches, but she doesn't roar. It's as though she hasn't heard this most terrible of all suggestions, that she accept her son-in-law's charity. She looks at her feet and says quietly, even meekly, "The waters. You don't know about the waters. The radioactivity enlarges the blood vessels. I read it."

Bernice, too, looks down at her mother's battered shoes. She knows she has a better pair in the closet, that she wore these for her, so that Bernice would be certain to see how poor, her struggles . . . Yet, even so, she can't help being sucked in a little by her mother's faith. It's something she gave up on years ago, and about more things in her life than her father's health. Nonetheless, it's her mother. Bernice can't stop herself from firing: "Your waters are a fraud, Mother, a cover for the gambling. Seymour says it got so bad a few years ago the mayor had to fire the entire police force. He also says everybody there has gonorrhea."

"Seymour, Seymour, Seymour. Where's Seymour, who loves your father so much?"

"Working, Mother. You know he'd be here if he wasn't working."

"So much love I'm choking."

Rachel sits, rests her hand on the kitchen table. Bernice takes a step backward, away from her mother. In the other room, her father booms.

They drove down there in a truck Manny, the junk dealer, lent them. Manny knew he'd never see it again, but it was the least he could do for Louie. Although even Manny, who'd always been the block's optimist, couldn't help thinking it would be more a hearse than a Dodge humpback in no time. Rachel drove. Louie sat beside her and told stories of the first time he laid eyes on her, at that ball at Baron von Rothschild's summer palace in Venice. How Rachel arrived in a while silk dress on the arm of Napoleon's other son, Felix, the blind one, the one history books ignore. And me a cobbler's son from the ghetto in Pilvishki sneaking a peek at you.

She got the café up and running in ten days. It so happened that a man was selling his place, a first bit of luck that made her think the potion of the waters was already working. Two afternoons a week, sometimes three times, when they had the money, she took him to Bathhouse Row. They went to the Quapaw because it was slightly cheaper than the other houses. It wasn't nearly as opulent as either the Maurice or the Buckstaff. But even the Quapaw was grander than anything they'd ever known in their lives, and Louie reveled in it. The vapors! The robes, the white towels, the Negro attendants in their impeccable shirts and scratchy bath mitts. Amid all the steam and the whiteness of the porcelain—who'd ever seen such white—he'd descend into the glory of that water. Tiny Louie scrubbed and dried. Louie from Roger's Park rubbed down by masseurs calling him Mister this and Mister that. He'd emerge from those baths a new man, singing the praises of the robber barons. The fat men, the fatter men. Who'd ever seen such obese men? Lord, these thieves know how to live! Bring back Hoover! I take back everything I ever said about their greedy child-killing hands! Hail the captains of industry! Hail the lying tycoons!

But he got worse. Faster than her worst nightmares foretold. Of course she knew he would, but she'd prayed to God, beseeched God. For once in my life, make me wrong about something.

Inside of six months in Arkansas, Louie could no longer hold a saucepan. He slept in a little bed in the kitchen by the stove. Rachel would sit in a chair beside the bed and watch him shake in his sleep. All night she'd watch him. She wrote to Bernice: "His body's too small for this. There isn't enough room for it and him." The only person they saw then was an old black man who lived in the basement. His name was Edwin Edwidge, a name that made Louie cackle and call him a liar. Edwin made his living sweeping sidewalks, but mostly, he told them, I'm a widower, which nobody pays me for. He often brought up coffee because he liked to listen to Louie's stories, and Louie couldn't get enough of the man because he always guffawed long and hard before a punch line had even entered Louie's head.

After she closed the café (she didn't wait for a buyer, just locked the door, didn't bother with a sign), they no longer had the money for the Quapaw. So Rachel took him to the government bathhouse, the free one. No velvet between your toes here. No copper tubs, no mosaic domes either. A flat low building, looked as if it was trying to hide. Rachel had never seen a building so ashamed of itself. She bit her lip and cursed God for creating America as she signed the pauper's oath on Louie's behalf. The ultimate humiliation of the poor: confessing it to a sneering clerk. She could have spit on his nose. And she'd wait outside on a wooden bench and watch the line that never slacked: shriekers, moaners, asthmatics, syphilitics, cripples, lepers. They dragged their feet across the sidewalk, they murmured to nobody. The parade of lunatics disgusted her. Rachel knew they couldn't help what had seized them, and yet she half believed what people sometimes said, that these unfortunates were paying for something. She didn't believe the quack about them being punished for crimes in a past life. No, something they did in this life had made every breath a hell on earth. She tried to close her eyes on them, but even in her own darkness she watched the parade shuffle by. Now my Louie joins their ranks.

She'd walk him home as he shivered, wrapped in blankets that dragged across the ground. He no longer tried to speak with his mouth—only with his eyes, and even they were exhausted. Just the two of them then, except for Edwin, who would come up and read Louie the newspaper. Rachel ordered him to read only the good news. This never took very long. After that, the three of them would sit for hours in the silence of Louie not being able to talk.

Finally a doctor at the Army-Navy Hospital told Rachel there was an operation he could try, a new procedure where you fixed one side and then the other, but the chances are fifty to one our old boy won't make it. Of course, on the other side of the coin, the doctor said. An awful slow goodbye.

Then—and this is the part people back home insisted for years that even Louie Shlansky, Fargo Avenue's greatest prevaricator, couldn't have cooked up with a straight face—she left him there. Abandoned him in Hot Springs, right there at the Army-Navy Hospital. The legend goes further: the woman drove back to Chicago in Manny's truck, alone.

The Como Hotel
Central Avenue, Hot Springs, Arkansas
5/25/40

Dear Seymour,

I spoke with Dr. Klemme today and he said he was coming along as good as could be expected under the circumstances—but that he's not "out of the woods just yet." He's doesn't know if Daddy's heart will able to stand this—only time will tell—that is the next 24 to 48 hours. He hasn't woken up yet to see she's not here. Of course you know that if he pulls through this he has to go through the same thing on the other side in two months. There is a man in the next bed who was operated on about ten days ago—but he's only had one side done so far. He's coming along fine, but he cries all the time because his nervous system is so upset. Of course there was another man who had the same operation about a week ago and he passed away the other night. He never came out of it at all. How are my two loves? Do they miss me? I miss them terribly. Make sure they make doody every day, and please be as much help to Mother as you can. I know she's never easy, but do try. Well, my mind is quite a muddle. Half the time I don't know whether I'm coming or going. This being away from each other may help us—who knows? Because you know what we do, Seymour? I watch my father die and I know. We squander. Write to me care of the Como Hotel.

All my love, B

Bernice brought his body home on the Ann Rutledge. A train named after Abraham Lincoln's girlfriend, a fact that would have sent her father into a convulsion of hosanas: You see, gentlemen, it was Mary Todd who poisoned Ann's venison. This was in 1863. I was Assistant Secretary of War, and yes, I signed the confession. But hear this! Countrymen! Romans! Ukrainians! I did it because the President asked me to—for the good of the country—and his marriage. How would it have looked? Mary Todd dragged away in shackles? Abe would have rather boxed a thousand Stonewall Jacksons than half a Mary Todd. It was I, I, Louie the First of Fargo Avenue, Roger's Park, who also saved the union.

Her mother never explained herself, and after a while Bernice stopped asking. Seymour said it was simple, that there was no mystery, that grief just undid already-loosened screws. Why dwell on it, Bernice? Leave her be. Why must you always dwell? They gave her the tiny guest room in the house on Lunt. Olivia carried her meals up there and listened to her. Rachel never spoke of the past, only the present. She talked of the way the light looked outside her window and of the temperature, how the cold felt on her arms. For two decades she rarely went out in the street. Philip was afraid of her; Esther told her friends that Grandma Rachel smelled like a wet raccoon. One day, in 1956, she finished her soup and died.

* * *

Bernice watches the February sun retreat from the bay window that looks out upon the slope of the ravine and the skeletal winter trees. The new house so huge and still around her, she can't help feeling like an intruder in its silence. And what kind of house is this if her mother doesn't live upstairs?

The vision appears slowly in the gray doom of the enormous window. It's a kitchen in Arkansas. A room she saw for less than an hour, so long ago now it happened to someone else, when she went to retrieve the papers, the photographs, the little furniture left to salvage. The sad black man who answered the door and didn't move his head when she told him the news. The dirty kitchen walls and the chair by the soiled bed. The filth. The filth is what startled her the most, that her mother had let it all go —

In the window her mother, barefoot and in a loose housedress, hovers over the bed. Her father is so shriveled under the blankets, his body is nothing more than a small lump. He's wearing a hat, a brown derby, that swallows his head. Bernice can't see his face. She watches her mother lean closer and sees everything. Her mother's bare feet, the grease-smudged walls, the cloudy window above the stove with its crack, a yellow fissure in the upper right corner. The lump that is her father, that hat. Feels her father's soft wheeze in the hollow of her mother's throat. *Tell me something, Louie, a lie, a bamboozle. Anything.* Her mother waits.

Acknowledgments

The author wishes to thank the James Michener–Copernicus Society of America and the Writers' Workshop at the University of Iowa for a generous fellowship, as well as Rhoda Pierce, Rob Preskill, and Dantia MacDonald for immeasurable faith and support.

About the Author

Peter Orner was born in Chicago in 1968. He has taught at a farm school in southern Africa, at Charles University in Prague, and at Miami University in Ohio. His stories have appeared in the *Atlantic Monthly*, *Southern Review*, *North American Review*, and other periodicals. One story from *Esther Stories* appears in *The Best American Short Stories 2001*, and another has received a Pushcart Prize. A graduate of Northeastern University School of Law and the University of Iowa Writers' Workshop, Orner currently teaches at the University of California, Santa Cruz.